SERAFINA CROLLA is a wife
who lives between Edinbur
province of Frosinone in Ita.y. born in Picinisco in the
foothills of the Abruzzi mountains, the daughter of a
shepherd, she has lived an unusual life.

The Wee Italian Girl

SERAFINA CROLLA

Luath Press Limited
EDINBURGH
www.luath.co.uk

First published 2018

This edition 2022

ISBN: 978-1-910022-46-7

Printed and bound by Clays Ltd, Bungay

Typeset in 12 point Sabon by Lapiz

Acknowledgements

I WOULD LIKE to thank Roland Ross, Monia Pacitti, Jennifer Alonzi, Maria Sarole, Luca Franchi and Nicola Sommerville for their help and computer skills. Also my copy editor, Louise Carolin, and Kavel Rafferty for her illustrations.

My son Remo and my daughter Maria Cristina for being the light of my life.

In memory of my father and mother, and all the rest who have gone to the village in the sky.

Foreword

THIS IS A story about an eight-year-old girl who lives in the mountains of central Italy, in the Abruzzi foothills. She is the daughter of a shepherd and lives with her family: her mother and father, her two brothers and her grandmother. They live on the mountains in the summer and move to the plains of Valle Comino in winter. This is the tale of her last summer in the village of Fontitune in the late 1950s, before she moved to Scotland with her family, leaving her beloved Nonna behind.

The girl still lives in Edinburgh with her family. She now has a granddaughter of her own who is eight years old. She tells her stories of when she was a child in Italy. 'Nonna, tell me a story,' her granddaughter often says.

So this book is for Erica.

FONTITUNE

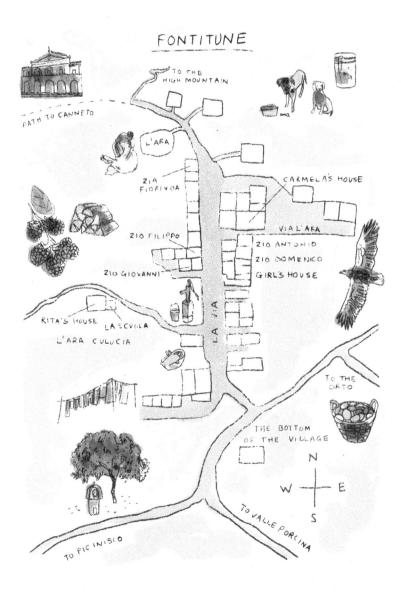

CHAPTER I

Once Upon a Time there was a Girl

ONCE UPON A time there was a girl who lived high up on the side of a mountain. Her name was Serafina. She lived in a village where there were no shops, not even a church, but there were about forty householders who made their living there. The village had one stony main road that went straight up; the houses were all attached in two long terraces with families on both sides.

The girl lived about halfway up, where there was a gate then a flight of steps on to a small *terrazza*, and then the front door. The house had three rooms: the first was the kitchen, at the back another room and then, up a flight of steep wooden steps and through a hatch, the bedroom that her mum and dad slept in. In these three rooms lived the girl, her mother and father, her *nonna* (grandmother) and two brothers, Fortunato and Vincenzo, one older and one younger.

Under the house there was the stable, which housed a grey horse, a grey pig, ten red speckled hens and one big strutting rooster. Outside of the stable there was a small courtyard where the hens scratched all day. This was the household of the girl.

I almost forgot; there were also two hundred sheep and three dogs, but most of the time they were in the high pasture in the mountains for the summer. The family would spend the summer in their home on the mountain and in winter they would go to the plains; the whole household would move. The plains were known as 'down-by', the mountain village, 'up-by'.

CHAPTER 2

A Springtime Return

IT WAS SPRINGTIME; the girl was on an old rusty truck which took the bends on the road at great throttle. They had been on the road travelling since early morning. The girl felt as if her body was out of control, being thrown this way and that as the truck roared uphill.

She was sitting in the cabin with her mother, Maria, who had her little brother Vincenzo on her lap at the front with the driver. Serafina was squeezed in behind her. In the back of the truck there were all their belongings, including a big cage full of hens, a table and chairs, beds, pots and pans. It was all covered with a great cover; they were going home.

Eventually after huffing and puffing, stops and starts and a great push, they came to a town and stopped. The girl looked out of the window and she could see the mountains of home. They still had snow at the top.

'Nearly there,' said her mother.

Her mother put her brother, who was sleeping, on the seat and got out of the truck. She went to the back of the truck to fetch a pail and rope and walked away.

The driver asked the girl if she wanted to get out while they waited for her mother, but she shook her head. She knew without being told that whenever her mother was not there she had to look after her younger brother. After a while her mother reappeared; she was leading a little pig who had its nose in a pail of corn. She went to the back of the truck, picked up the squealing pig and put it in, tied the rope to the side of the truck, put the pail of corn in front of its nose and left the pig happily eating. The driver jumped in and they were off again: down, down they went until they came to a high road; from the window, she could see her mountains.

Eventually it grew dark, and started to rain. She fell asleep.

'Wake up.' Her mother shook her; they had arrived.

The rain was still falling. She could hardly stand. She was so tired. She cried. Her brother cried. The pig squealed. Her mother took her by the hand, she carried the baby and pulled the pig on a lead. They had to walk up the steep, rutted road. They came to the house. The pig was put in the stable, the children on the doorstep; her mother covered them both with a blanket and told them to stay there until she came back. They sat on the steps and cried; wet, cold and hungry.

It seemed an age before her mother came back. She appeared with the cage of hens on her head. There were other people too who were carrying things. Then her mother produced a big black key and opened the door, quickly taking them to the back room where she stripped them of their clothes, dressing them in dry vests and pants, and put them to bed. Serafina's head touched the pillow – she was asleep.

In the morning she woke up and went into the kitchen where she found her nonna, and most of their things piled up in the middle of the floor. Her nonna was heating milk on the open fire. She cut thick slices of bread off the huge round loaf, put them on a dish and poured the hot milk on top, sprinkled them with sugar, and put it in front of the girl. The girl wolfed it down.

She went outside on the small terrace and looked at all the familiar things. She felt so happy, but did not know why she was happy. Now all she had to do was wait for her dad, her brother Fortunato, the grey horse, two hundred sheep, and three dogs to arrive and they would all be at home. They were making the return trip to the village on foot and it would take them three days, following centuries-old tracks.

CHAPTER 3

Summer School

WITHIN A WEEK, all the families of the village had made the return journey to their homes in the mountains. The girl was playing from morning till night. So much to catch up on! Her cousins and friends, all the children of the village, seemed to have grown overnight and it took a while before she got used to them being the same people she had left in the winter.

Her best friend was her cousin Rita. They were the same age, although you would not think it to look at them as Serafina was a big strapping girl and Rita was small and very thin. Rita lived just outside of the village in a new house. It was called *L'ara Cullucia*. The girl went there often, either to stay and play or to call Rita to come to play in the village if there was a good game going on. This day, the girl was going to see her uncle, Rita's father, to give him a message from her father. When she walked into the kitchen there were people seated round the table. Strangers! A beautiful young woman.

The girl could not take her eyes off the young woman's lips, they were so red. There was also a man dressed in a blue uniform. She stood by the table, waiting to give her uncle the message from her father, trying not to interrupt. After a while her uncle asked what she wanted, so she gave him the message. She then walked into the courtyard, where Rita was with all the others. She understood that the woman with the red lips was coming to teach the children of the village. The schoolroom was to be in one of the rooms of her uncle's old house.

The day came to go to school. Mother gave her a bag with a jotter and pencils and she was pushed out of the door and told to be good and listen to the teacher. She was nervous and shy. Would the woman with red lips be strict? Would she have a stick? Yes she was, and yes she did. One of her favourite punishments was one strap on each hand for being late for class, and more if late again. Not having homework done earned a child two straps on each hand; more if necessary. For the big boys who said anything about her red lips and laughed, their torture was to kneel on a handful of corn in a corner, facing the wall. If they dared to turn around, five minutes was added to the time.

The girl had seen big boys cry. She had the face of an angel, their teacher, but she was a she-devil with red lips. She was very strict. Every morning there was a hand inspection to see if they were clean and the nails cut; a neck inspection; a head inspection; it went on. Always to greet her with, '*Buongiorno, signorina maestra.*' They had to endure her presence in the village until the end of July when summer school closed for the year. Then they said, '*Arrivederci, signorina maestra,*' and hoped never to see her again.

CHAPTER 4

Communion

ALL OF THE children who were eight years old that year had to have their First Holy Communion. The girl knew this already because at home, in a white box, was a beautiful frothy white dress, which her mother had bought in the winter in preparation for this event. The dress was ready, the girl was not.

In preparation for the big day the children had to learn the catechism. To do this they had to go to the convent in Picinisco, where the nuns taught them all they had to know. To know by heart the *Ave Maria*, *Padre Nostro*, *Credo*, and so on. Also the mortal sins that would send them straight to hell. How to confess everything to a priest, and be saved this terrible fate. The nuns put the fear of God into you. The girl would have nightmares, but she thought that it was worth it, thinking of the white dress. On this day, the girl hurried home when school was over; she quickly ate her pasta with tomato sauce, with lots of pecorino cheese on top, and changed into a clean cotton dress.

'Wash your hands and face,' called her mother, which she did. Her mother then gave her fifty *lira*, and off she went. Rita was waiting for her at the turning to her house. Soon other boys and girls who were also going to the convent in Picinisco joined them. The walk to the town would take them about an hour; they had to hurry, the lesson started at two o'clock. It was hot and the afternoon sun was fierce, the road rough and stony, but at least it was all downhill. It would be much harder coming home, but at least then they could take their time and the sun would not be so hot. When they turned the last bend on the road, the town of Picinisco was visible before them and soon they were there.

The convent was close to the edge of the town. The girl, her friend Rita and the others all went in. Sister Teresa was waiting for them and also for children from other villages. The class was almost full with children from Picinisco. A big rough boy made a sound like a sheep, and the town children all laughed. The girl did not know why this was funny. When the class was over, it was then the best part of the day. They would walk down to the *piazza*, take a huge drink from the ice-cold water of the public fountain and then think what to spend their money on.

For the girl, it was difficult to decide what to have. She wanted everything. First she wanted a small bar of chocolate, then she would see one of the children with a yellow and white ice cream cone, which made her mouth water. The ice cream cost fifty *lira*; she could have two ice lollies for fifty *lira*, or three lollipops. She walked about trying to decide. While she walked about, her friend Carmela followed her closely. Every step the girl took, Carmela would take too, until in a fit of anger the girl shouted, 'Go away, I'm going to have an ice cream,' and dashed into the shop.

When she walked out, she was licking a rainbow-coloured ice lolly. Carmela was there waiting, with her eyes big and sad. The girl gave her the other ice lolly she'd bought with her fifty *lira*, which made Carmela jump up and down with joy. They set off for home, trying to make their ice lollies last as long as possible but they were soon gone. A boy had bought a lollipop and was still happily sucking its sweet stickiness, which made her think that perhaps she had made the wrong choice. Still, there was always tomorrow.

It was the feast of Corpus Domini; the girl had been hearing this all week from snatches of conversations she heard from grown-ups. Sister Teresa said that it meant the body of Christ, which they were to receive on their First Holy Communion. When the big day arrived the girl felt so excited; all over the village there was preparation. In her house it was the same.

Everyone's hair was washed and dried in the sun; a chicken killed and cooked over an open fire. Early in the morning, they stood in the tub and got washed all over, even the boys. They hated this more than anything. All the family were clean and dressed in their best clothes, a basket with their dinner packed. Last of all, to make sure she would not get it dirty, the white box was taken out and the beautiful dress admired by all.

Dress on! A little ring of flowers and a veil put on her head, white socks and dainty white shoes, which hurt her big rough feet, and then, most important of all, a lace-covered bag with a loop for a handle, which she put on her arm.

Off they went in turn, father holding Vincenzo's hand and looking handsome in his white shirt. Mother with a basket on her head, carrying dinner. Nonna also with a basket on her head. Big brother Fortunato already by the gate, dying to go off with his friends. And last of all the girl, bursting with pure joy.

When they got to the bottom there was Middiuccio, the taxi man. He was there if anyone wanted to be taken to town; 'So-much per person.' The girl's father took the basket off his mother-in-law's head and put it on the rack on the top of the car and he paid the man.

'You go in the car, Mamma, the walk is too much for you,' he said to his mother-in-law.

'No. I can walk, I'll go slow,' she said.

She did not want the money to be wasted on her. But her son-in-law insisted and she was seated in the car along with other people. Family groups soon got together and chatted and laughed as they walked to Picinisco.

The girl was left behind; walking in the long dress was not easy, her shoes were hurting and she soon got a blister. She could see her mother way up in front looking back for her. They were almost at the bend where you could see the town. Her mother shouted to her to hurry. The girl ran to catch up and as she did this, she put her foot in the frill of her dress and it tore. She looked at it and could not believe it, she started to cry bitterly. Her mother looked at her dress: 'Could you not be careful?' she said. She then unpinned two or three safety pins, which she always had on her person, and pinned the frill back in place on the dress. 'There,' she said. 'You can't see it so stop crying.'

Her father looked at the blister and patted her on her head. He took the shoe, put it on a large stone at the side of the road and with another stone bashed the shoe and made it soft. He then took out his handkerchief, tore off a bit of it to make a little padding and put it on the blister. Sock on, shoe on again and happiness returned.

At the convent, the Sisters lined up the children two by two; the girl held on tight to Rita's hand. Girls at the front, boys at the back. Parents and family also in pairs. They walked in procession through the *piazza* to the church. Once there, Mass was said and Holy Communion received. This was what the girl, Rita, Carmela and all the rest were waiting for. Free from the Sisters and from family, they made their way through the narrow, cobbled lane back to the *piazza*. Once there, they were to take a drink from the fountain, to wash down the Body of Christ, which they did. The girl looked around, the *piazza* was full of people. She went to her Uncle Domenico, Rita's father, took his hand, kissed it and said, 'Corpus Domini, Zio.' Her uncle put his hand on her head to bless her, then he put his hand in his pocket and gave her one hundred *lira*. She said, 'Thank you.' She smiled from ear to ear. She plunged her money into the lace bag and off she went to repeat the action with all her other uncles and aunties and big cousins and all the other *zii* of the village. To the girl everyone in the village was a *zio* or *zia*, an uncle or an aunt.

Late afternoon. Baskets empty. Father still in the tavern drinking. Mother, Nonna, Zia sitting in the shade chatting, watching the small children. Big boys and girls running about playing and grown-up boys and girls laughing together, sitting in groups. Young men sitting with their *fidanzate* alone, *a fare l'amore* and all the eight-year-old children counting their money under the old oak tree.

CHAPTER 5

Going to Feed the Dog

BEFORE THE FLOCK of sheep could be moved to the high pastures on the mountains, the snow had to melt. So until that happened, the animals were grazed round about the village. At night they were penned up in the fields, to keep them safe and so they would add manure to the soil, ready to plough up when they were moved up to the mountains.

It was Serafina's job to take food for the dogs wherever they happened to be. In the house there would be a 'dog pail' with leftover pasta and scraps of food, and some bones if they were lucky. The girl would take the pail and also a jam jar with a lid, with a string round the rim to form a handle. It was just getting dark as she set off. As she walked up the road other children, also with pails and jam jars, were walking up the road, also going to feed their dogs. Soon, little groups of children would get together. They would hurry, they had to be there just at the right time. Twilight was best.

'I'm going to get more than you.'

'No, you are not.'

'Yes, I am.'

'How much do you bet I am going to get more than you?'

And that was more or less the gist of the conversation all the way up.

Just as they got over the brow of the hill, the dogs that were waiting for them bounded down the track to meet them. No, they were not to get their food until they were at their place, beside their flock. The children hurried on, wanting to get their task done. The girl greeted and petted her three dogs, especially Caponero, who was her favourite. She divided the food between the three dogs, making sure they all got a share. By this time it was dark and the illumination had begun. Thousands of fireflies: their lights winking on and off, dancing in the air. The children darting here and there, catching as many as they could and putting them in their jam jars.

Eventually they were tired and made their way home, each with a lantern of light in their hand.

'Mine is brighter than yours. I bet I have more than you.'

'You think so? We'll go and count them.'

The glow from the jars illuminated their steps back down the stony track.

CHAPTER 6

Blind Man's Buff

AT LAST THE snow on the peaks of the mountains melted and underneath, in the high pastures, lay a rich green grass for the sheep to graze on. So the time had come to take them to their summer home and this was no easy task. The sheep had to be counted and marked. They had to be milked and then the milk weighed. This had to be done in front of the shepherds to make sure there was no cheating because from the weight of the milk they would calculate how much cheese and *ricotta* each was entitled to.

When all this was done, the sheep would all be herded together and taken up to the mountains. Then the shepherds would have to come to an agreement as to how many days at a time each man would have to stay up the mountain, to graze the sheep, to milk them, to make the cheese, to guard them from wolves. The more sheep you had, the longer you stayed, usually seven to ten days at a time.

One day, the girl's father came home from his stint up the mountain. Usually when this happened, her mother would make especially nice food and have hot water ready for him to wash and shave. The girl's mother had made egg pasta with sausage and meatballs in tomato sauce. The children loved this and enjoyed every mouthful. After the meal, little brother Vincenzo went for his afternoon nap. Her mother and father went upstairs and closed the hatch and the girl and her older brother were larking about, playing.

Now, Serafina's father had decided to have the small *terrazza* outside the front door enlarged, so that they could eat outside. The children could play on it and there would also be more space under it for storage. This was in the process of being built and was just about finished, the only thing still to do was the bannister. The children were playing on it, and getting a little bored, they decided to play 'blind man's buff'. It was Serafina's turn to be the blind man. Her hands outstretched, she felt about for Fortunato. He had so much extra space on the new *terrazza* and was making it hard for her to catch him.

Her last memory was of being on the *terrazza* with her arms outstretched and laughing. And the next, walking down the road with her arm in a sling.

She was going to see a special Zia who was a bone setter. Zia Teresa was an old woman who was good at massage and pushing bones back into place, and that was just what the girl was going there for. She had stepped off the *terrazza*, hit her head, passed out and also it turned out, broken her arm. Her mother's screams brought the whole village running. Everyone thought the girl had died.

CHAPTER 7

Tied to the Table

THE GIRL'S FATHER would spend ten days on the mountain and ten days at home, where he and his wife would do the other chores which had to be done because, apart from the flock of sheep, they also had plots of land on which they would grow wheat enough for bread and homemade pasta for the whole year. Enough corn to feed the chickens and for *polenta*. Barley, and plenty of it for the horse. Potatoes grew on the allotment on the mountain.

And they were lucky enough that on one of their plots of land, there was a small spring of water and there the girl's mother, Maria, had an *orto* (vegetable patch) which was the envy of everyone in the village. She grew tomatoes, cucumbers, peppers, salad things. Sometimes, if it was extra hot, she would grow melons. The only downfall was sometimes, after all the hard work she had put in producing them, during the night the vegetables would be stolen. Not by the people of her village, because no one touched anything in the village. All doors were open. It was 'someone from Picinisco', or so the girl heard.

They worked hard, but they were lucky that they had Maria's mother at home. Nonna would do all the cooking for the family, and the cooking for Mr Pig because he also got a hot meal, feed the chickens and look after the children.

Every time they went out they would say to Serafina: 'Now help Nonna, don't go out to play all day.'

So the girl would say to her grandmother: 'Will I fetch water, will I sweep the floor, have you enough firewood?!'

As soon as she thought everything was done she would disappear before her nonna could ask her to play with and look after Vincenzo, because then she would have to stay at home or take Vincenzo with her, which was not much fun.

One day she returned home for her midday meal. As soon as she stepped into the house her father made to take off his belt to give her a licking and he said to her: 'What did I say to you about staying at home to help Nonna?'

Now, Serafina was not really scared of her father because the action with the belt never really got any further than that, but this time the belt actually came out of his trousers. She ran to hide behind her nonna.

Her nonna put a protecting hand on her and said to her son-in-law: 'Let her be, this time. I'm sure she will try harder from now on.' Relief; the belt was put back in his trousers and they all sat down to eat.

Next morning, everyone was getting ready for the day. Her father went into the stable to harness the horse, and came back upstairs with a rope in his hands. He said to Serafina: 'We will see if you go out today.' He took one end of the rope and tied it to the kitchen table, and the other end on the girl's ankle. 'That will make you stay at home, and Mamma don't you untie her.'

The worst thing about it was that the rope was just long enough that she could walk outside the door, where she could see the other children as they called to her to play from the street.

CHAPTER 8

Mother Is Never Wrong

SERAFINA WAS WITH her mother, her father doing his shift on the mountain looking after the herd of sheep. So, her mother was on her own in the fields, hoeing the rows of corn, removing weeds and grass, so that the corn would have a better chance to grow strong and tall. She had to be careful because mixed with the corn seeds there were also a few pumpkin seeds and chickpea seeds, which would grow in the shade of the tall corn plants. Her mother Maria had to be careful to take up just the weeds.

The girl was in a clearing in the woods that was on the side of the plot of land. The clearing had been made years ago by folk who came from down-by, who made charcoal. Serafina was looking for wild forest strawberries, she had a stick with which she would beat the vegetation to scare away snakes and other beasts.

The girl could hear her mother talking to Zio Pietro, the man who owned the plot of land next to hers. The girl went to have a look.

Her mother was standing with the hoe in her hand, having a heated argument with the old man. Zio Pietro was shouting at her mother. The child hurried to her mother's side holding the stick tight in her fist.

'What are you saying, you stupid woman?' he said to her mother. 'This land has always been like this, I think I should know, my family has owned this plot of land for generations, you have had your piece for only a few years. Get out of the way and let me do my work!' He started to dig up the earth near to Maria's feet.

Maria had noticed that her field seemed to be getting less every year. She stood her ground; with both hands she leaned on the hoe. She was very angry. 'You have moved at least two paces into my land,' she shouted at him. 'Every year you take a bit more.'

'Get out of my way, woman, you don't know what you are talking about, I will show you!' And he picking up a sickle, Pietro strode over to the edge of the field. Maria followed him and the girl followed her mother.

He hacked away at some bushes with the sickle, then stood back. 'There!' he said as he defiantly stood back and pointed to the marker.

Maria looked in amazement, she could see the orange marker. Serafina looked at her mother; she had been wrong, her mother was never wrong.

Maria looked quizzically with her hoe in hand, she stood peering this way and that. She was looking for something. She could not find what she was looking for until shifting some scrub and bushes... 'You bastard,' she shouted at Pietro. 'You have moved the marker.' She looked as if she was going to have a fit. Serafina was getting upset to see her mother so angry and started to cry.

'There,' she cried as she pointed to a metal spike, which you could see just peeping from the ground.

'That is where the marker should be, you have moved it. My husband put that metal spike next to the marker when we bought this piece of land, how dare you do such a thing, you ignorant old man!'

'What? Are you telling me, a man of more than twice your age, that this is not the right marker? THIS is the official orange marker, you and your husband have put that spike into my land,' insisted Pietro, angrily.

The girl looked on as the old man lifted the hand in which he held the sickle and made as if he was going to attack her mother and before she knew what she was doing with the stick, which she held tight in her hand, she struck a hard blow on the man's knees.

Her mother pulled her back to stop her from striking him another blow.

The man looked at the child with disbelief and put his hands to his knees. Maria took the girl by the hand and walked away. 'We will see about this, we will call the law, we will call the surveyor and you will pay for the expense,' she shouted.

Just then, Zio Filippo was walking by to go to his plot of land. Maria called him: 'Zio Filippo, could you come here and look at this, you could be witness that he has moved the marker?'

Zio Filippo was not keen to go and have a look, he did not want to get involved because these quarrels about plots could go on for years. Every inch of land was precious, people with large families had to struggle to grow enough to make bread for the year.

Maria begged him to take a look. He could see how upset she was and he took pity on the crying child by her side, so he went to see what it was all about.

When the girl's father came home, his wife told him what had happened. He went into a rage; he wanted to go and have it out with the man. Her mother calmed him down and said to him that he could not go and beat up an old man. Better to send him a message to put back the marker where it should be or they would go to the law.

A few weeks later the girl again went with her mother and father to the same plot of land. She was sitting in the clearing eating tiny sweet strawberries. The clearing was like a round, enclosed green room with dense vegetation meeting overhead. Through the trunks of the trees she could see her parents side by side, each with a spade, digging up the strip of earth they had reclaimed as their own.

Zio Pietro had insisted that he had not moved the marker and the land was his, so her father had called the surveyor to measure the plot of land and, sure enough, he found that the marker had been moved. Zio Pietro had to pay the surveyor's fees, plus a fine for touching the marker. The girl's father wanted compensation but that would involve going to court. Her father knew that when you began a court case it might never end. It could go on for years. So he let it go. But from then on, whenever he mentioned Pietro's name it always ended with a '*che gli possa star all'infern*' – 'may he rot in hell.'

CHAPTER 9

Fortunato Falling Off the Horse

AFTER THE EXCITEMENT of the Holy Communion, the children of the village settled down to long days of playing. The girls played together, the boys had their own games. Sometimes they got together to play some rough games that big boys enjoyed more than the younger children.

One of the games that the older boys liked to play with the younger children was called 'sheep' and for some reason they always wanted to play this when there were no adults about. The game was to round the children up into a pretend pen. They were to be the sheep. The big boys would take turns at being either the sheepdog, the Master or the Ram.

When the children were rounded up by the dog and Master, the Ram would also go in the pen where he would jump on the children, pretending to sniff their bottoms. He would chase the children and there would be a pile-up with the Ram on top. Squeals of laughter could be heard all over the village.

If a parent of one of the younger children would happen to be passing, he would bark at the big boys to leave the children alone and not to play such rough games. Then he would shout at his own children to get home. Somehow she felt that it was not nice to play this game, but the girl did not know why.

Apart from playing, the children, even the youngest, had jobs to do at home. One of the tasks that the boys had to do was to look after the family's horse or donkey or mule. They had to take it to the fountain to drink, feed it barley when it came home after working all day, rub it down and cover it with a blanket when it came home in a sweat. When their horse had no work to do, the girl's older brother Fortunato would take her to pasture on the hillsides where she would roam free until late afternoon.

All the families in the *paese* (village) had either a donkey or a mule. There were only a handful of horses in the village and their horse Peppa was the only one that was grey; the others were a rough, dull brown. Peppa was Fortunato's pride and joy. She was tall and sleek. He would brush and comb her blonde tail and mane. Peppa would flick her tail and look at the boy with pleasure.

The boys that had a horse would meet at the bottom of the hill, they would get on their horses and ride bareback to the pastures. More often than not, a race would develop to see who could get there first, and it would be the same on the journey home. Fortunato liked to race his horse as he would win most days but there was always a fierce battle for second place.

One day, the girl had gone home to have her midday meal of *pasta e fagioli* (pasta and cannellini beans). The dishes had been left to soak in the basin. The doors and windows were closed to keep the heat of the afternoon out. Fortunato had gone to see to the horse and bring her home. Serafina went to lie down beside her sleeping little brother, she kissed his flushed, sweaty cheeks. She was tossing and turning;

all she could hear was the clicking of knitting needles. Her nonna was sitting in the cool kitchen, knitting woollen vests for the family for the winter.

She could hear also the crickets on the long grass outside. They had gone mad, the sound was so loud; how was it possible that such small animals made such a loud sound! Eventually she fell asleep. It seemed only moments that she had slept when she heard the door pushed open. Her cousin Pierino crying, shouting, 'Zia Maria, Zia Maria!' Her mother came bounding down the wooden steps to see what had happened.

'Zia,' he said, 'Fortunato has fallen off the horse, he has split his head open, there is blood everywhere! He is going to die,' he wailed.

'Where is he now?' her mother asked, trying to keep calm. She grabbed a couple of clean towels and ran out. She flew down the stony street. The girl followed her until they came to the bottom of the village, where she could see a crowd of people. Her mother ran screaming, now fearing the worst. Fortunato was sitting on a chair, his head wrapped in a bloody cloth. Relief – he was alive. He had a deep cut in his head but he would live. With all that blood, it looked worse than it was.

Maria removed the bloody cloth and replaced it with a clean towel that she had brought with her. What was she to do? The hospital was in Atina, half a days walk away. Zio Stefano said he would send his son on a horse to Picinisco to get a doctor, or get Middiuccio in his car to take him to the hospital. 'No,' said the girl's mother, 'we have to stop the flow of the blood now. Help! Help me to get him to my brother-in-law Giovanni, he will know what to do.' He had been a sergeant in the army and attended to wounded soldiers during the war.

'Please help me to get him there,' she begged. 'Serafina, you run ahead and tell Zio Giovanni what has happened, that we are bringing Fortunato to him, and on the way tell Nonna he is going to be alright.'

With Zio Stefano on one side of the chair and his son on the other they raised it up with the boy still on it and started up the road with a crowd of people following. Meanwhile the girl in a frenzy had run all the way to her uncle's house and pushed open the door; she knew that her uncle would be napping. She shouted up the stairs: 'Zio Giovanni, Fortunato has fallen off the horse, he has split his head open, he is going to die, they are bringing him here.' The girl watched; the first thing her uncle did was stir the embers in the fireplace, put some firewood on to bring up a flame, put a metal stand on the fire, fill a pot with water, put three eggs in it and put them on the fire to cook.

The girl looked on with astonishment, this was no time to cook his food; her brother was hurt, he could die, and just at the thought of it she started to cry.

She could hear her mother, everyone was talking. The crowd had grown. They were outside the house. Zio Stefano and his son were sweating from the effort of carrying Fortunato up the steep road. Zio Giovanni looked at the wound and said to her mother that it was not too bad, nothing to worry about. Serafina watched as her uncle set to work. He cut the hair away from the wound, washing it with the boiling water he had cooked the eggs in. Then, with needle and thread, he sewed the wound up. Fortunato, screaming all the while.

After this was done he started to peel the boiled eggs. What? This was no time to eat eggs. She watched. With pincers he carefully pulled away the white lining between the shell and egg and delicately put this on the stitched-up cut. When he had finished, he put a bandage round the boy's head and all was done.

'There,' he said. 'All done, he will be alright.' And he was.

CHAPTER 10

Potato Harvest

THE SUMMER WAS long and hot, and to the girl it seemed to go on forever. The summer school had closed. Daily treks to Picinisco over, the First Holy Communion a thing of the past. For the children it was playtime! But the children were also asked to help with household tasks, not only their own family's but also those of their *zios* and *zias*. It was thought very rude to say no. With aunties and uncles it was mostly to deliver messages to other people of the village, or to find children and tell them that they were wanted at home.

One day, the girl was sitting on Peppa, the grey horse. She was holding on tight. Her mother had told her to not let go as they made off. The mare knew her way up the steep stony track. Her mother was behind the horse, holding onto its tail to get a little help as they walked up the mountain.

From her vantage point on the horse, the girl could see the narrow track that led to the great beech forest and beyond that the mountains. Down below she could see the village, and from up there she could also see Picinisco and the valley below. Once they had passed the forest, they came to a green grassy plain between the forest and the high mountains, and it was here that the cows, calves and horses were free to roam all summer, eating the sweet young grass.

They went on until they came to a cabin that was a refuge for people who got stuck in bad weather. On the flat, fertile land around the cabin were allotments. And this was what they had come for. Mother took a sack and a spade off the horse and made her way to her patch of ground. She told the girl to take Peppa for a drink in a ditch where there was water and to let the horse crop the grass roundabout.

The woman set to work, digging up the rich dark soil and beautiful big red potatoes would pop up. She soon had a sack full of potatoes and called Serafina to bring the horse. The girl led the horse to her mother. Peppa was soon loaded up with the sack which was tied on securely with rope. The mother put the lead of the horse in her daughter's hand, slapped Peppa on the rump. 'Be careful,' she shouted as girl and horse set off for home.

Peppa knew her own way home, she chose her footing carefully, taking the zig-zag route rather than the straight. It was as if she knew she was carrying an important load and had to be careful. She was following her mother's instructions. The girl followed the mare, just occasionally encouraging the horse: 'Wow, take it easy now, there is no rush.'

Eventually they got home. Nonna was there in the little courtyard; she untied the load and let it slide off the horse to the ground. Serafina took Peppa for a drink at the fountain, then led her to the shade of the stable and gave her some hay. Both horse and girl had a rest. After a while, her nonna helped the girl back on to the horse, told her to hold on tight and away they went for another load. When she got to the allotment the girl's mother had another sackful of potatoes ready. Other people who were there doing the same thing came to help her to load the sack on Peppa's back but this time both mother and daughter followed the horse home.

They would come again and again until the job was done. After a few days, Maria, her mother and Serafina sat round the great heap of potatoes and sorted them out. Bruised, green or very small ones were for the pig; nice but damaged ones were to be used right away; small perfect round ones kept for next year's seed. The biggest and best potatoes were for the family and enough to last the year, if they were carefully stored.

CHAPTER 11

Playing with the Boys

THE CHILDREN OF the mountain village made their own games. They played, laughed and sometimes they would throw stones. The stones were always at hand, you just had to bend down, pick up and throw. One day, Rita and Serafina were playing one of their favourite games. They were playing at being mummy.

Now, they did not have dolls to play with but they would make their own: a cloth wrapped around a potato would be the head and a towel would be the body and off they went with this bundle in their arms. They would ask each other if the baby was being good, if it needed changing and so on. If it was hungry they would sit down and breastfeed their babies. Now this was fine. They enjoyed the game, Carmela and other girls would join them in their play as well.

But best of all was when they played with real babies. The girl and Rita both had their favourite. Serafina would go to a young couple who lived next to her house: Rosina and Giuseppe. They had a little boy; his name was Fernando. She would say to Rosina: 'Can I take Fernando out? I will look after him!' Rosina would give the boy to Serafina, she would put him on her hip and she would carry the boy about, pretending she was his mummy.

Rita had her own favourite. His name was Paolo. He was the same size as Serafina's baby. They would get together and play the same games but this time with real babies. 'My baby is nicer than yours, look he has nice curly hair. My baby can say Mummy.' They would tickle their babies and make them laugh and so on. They were sitting down pretending to feed their babies: their blouses opened, the little boys' faces pressed into their flat bosoms. They had put a hankie over each boy's head because that was what they had seen real mothers do. Some did not bother but some did. The girls thought that it was much nicer to do this as you did not want everyone to see your breasts.

They were sitting down doing this, when Pierino, the girl's cousin, stopped to talk to them to see what they were doing. He laughed, then he started to tease them: 'Let me see your tits then, come on, let me see them!' Then he pulled the hankie away revealing Serafina's flat chest and he laughed even harder.

The girl got up, the stone already in her hand and threw it. Now, the children were quite good at this. The stone hit him right on his brow, above his right eye. He started to howl and said that he was going to tell his father. As he passed the girl's house, his uncle Raffaele, the girl's father, was standing on the *terrazza*. He asked Pierino what was the matter, why was he crying.

'Serafina hit me with a stone.'

When the girl went home in time for *pranzo* (the midday meal), her father, with that withering look of his asked her why she had thrown a stone at Pierino's head. The girl explained what had happened and started to cry, thinking there was going to be a row. Instead, her father kissed her gently and said if anyone did anything like that again, to throw two stones instead.

CHAPTER 12

Just a Bad Dream

THE GIRL'S DAD had come down from doing his ten days turn in the mountains looking after the great flock of sheep. When Raffaele walked into the house, he was dirty with sweat, his skin tanned, his hair flat against his head. Mother laughed when she saw him. She had hot water ready to shave his long stubble; she had a change of clothes ready, his shoes greased and shiny. He would sit and take off his *cioce* (leather lace-up sandals), which he wore when he was on the mountain, and put on his shiny shoes. But first he would wash all over.

The children would go out to play. They would return when it was time to eat. By this time, the girl's father was clean and fresh. He looked handsome in his white shirt. His eyes so blue in his tanned face.

The family would sit down to eat food that her mother had prepared. Cold foods because it was so hot at this time of year: cold fried peppers; a salad of tomatoes and cucumber; *pasta al pomodoro fresco* and always wine and cold water. After dinner was over, the children were encouraged to go out to play. 'Go to Zio Domenico. See what is going on there, go to play with Rita,' Mother said to the girl.

The girl started to go to *L'ara Cullucia*. She dragged her feet, it was so hot. It was one of these days when

43

not a leaf stirred, the air shimmered, the dogs all asleep in the shade. When she got to her uncle's place, the house was in deep silence. Her uncle asleep on the bench with his mouth open. The boys asleep under the shade of a tree in the courtyard. She went upstairs to Rita's room; she was asleep with her sisters Carmela and Concetta.

The girl toyed with the thought of getting in beside them but there was already three in the bed, it would be too hot if she got in as well. She decided to go home. She pushed open the door of her house; inside was dark and cool. She took a drink of cold water, opened the door to the back room where her little brother was asleep on the bed. She kissed him and lay down beside him. She looked up the steps to the hatch of her mother and father's room. It was closed; they must be sleeping.

She could hear the bed squeaking. It was not the usual sound of the movement of the springs when one moved in the bed but a squeak, squeak, squeak, like the ticking of a clock. She listened to the rhythmic noise which was putting her to sleep. The girl woke with a start; she heard what sounded like a scream of pain, coming from the room upstairs. She sat up and listened.

'Are you alright, Mum?' she shouted.

After a while her mother answered, 'Yes I am fine, just a bad dream.'

CHAPTER 13

Doing the Washing

IN THE SMALL house that the girl lived in, there was not much housework to do apart from cooking and washing dishes. The floor was stone, not much furniture and few ornaments adorned the interior. The fire made a mess, you had to sweep away the ashes and sometimes it would smoke, but that was the realm of her grandmother. She was very good at keeping the fire going so that it would never actually go out. At night, she would bury the embers in the ash. In the morning she would dig out the embers add a few twigs on top, then she would blow in her *sisciature*, a long iron tube with a flat end, and the twigs would burst into flames, then she'd put wood on top and that was it: fire on!

Sometimes there were no embers, they had all burned away, and there were no matches. Then the girl was sent to her zio Luigi's house with a metal shovel, to get some embers from his fire to relight the one at home. Sometimes other people would come to her house to 'borrow embers'. They would simply look to see whose chimney was smoking.

The washing of clothes and bed-linen was done at the public fountain at the bottom of the village. Mother would put all the clothes in a great big blue basin, with a great slab of homemade soap and a flask of bleach. She would put it on her head and set off for the fountain.

The girl would follow with a small basin on her head. Her mother did not hold on to her basin because she was so used to carrying things on her head that it was second nature to her. Her balance was perfect, graceful even, but the girl could not do this; she tried letting go of her basin but a series of crashes ensued.

When they got to the fountain there were other women doing their washing. The water came gushing out of a tap on the wall at one end. It flowed into a cement tank and when that was full it would overflow into another tank, and so on. There were four tanks in all for doing the washing. At the other end there was another tap which flowed into a large trough, and this was for the animals to drink from.

When you were washing your clothes there were certain rules to follow. At the fourth tank you did your dirtiest clothes: rub soap in, rinse, soap in, rinse. In the third tank you washed all your household things and Sunday's clothes and so on; rub soap in, rinse. In the second tank you rinsed things which you had washed and put to steep in bleach. Last of all, in the first tank, where the water was cleanest, you did your last rinse.

The girl's mother went to the bottom of the line of women and started to wash. The girl tried to squeeze in beside her to wash things in her basin. She loved the coolness of the water splashing all over her. There was a lot of chatting and laughing among the women: washing of clothes was a very social thing.

Sometimes, when a man came to water his horse or other animals, the women would fall silent; they were talking about things that could not be said in front of men. Other times, when young single men came to water their animals, there would be even more talking and laughing and if there were any young girls present there would be a lot of teasing from the married women. The young girls would blush, look at the young men from under their eyelashes and laugh.

If a man liked a girl, he would hang around until she had finished her washing so that he could walk her home.

There was a lot of larking about at the fountain, the girls would look for any excuse to do the washing and the boys liked to go there because the girls were there. Sometimes, though, the boys were chased away because the women did not like to wash their knickers and such in front of them. The boys knew this and would come to water their beasts even when they did not have to. Everyone had a good laugh at the fountain.

The girl had been watching all of the goings on but she was just interested in doing her washing. Eventually her mother was at the top of the line, rinsing all her clothes in the clean sparkling water. She put all her washing in the blue basin to take home and hang to dry on her *terrazza*. The basin was much heavier now, so the other women helped her to lift the basin onto her head. Serafina asked if they could help her to put her basin on her head, and they all laughed as they did so.

CHAPTER 14

The Water Carrier

SERAFINA WALKED TO the fountain to fill the straw-covered flasks with drinking water, because it was her job to make sure that the water was fresh. The trouble was that it would not stay fresh for very long, because the days were so hot, with the August sun fierce in the sky. So, she spent all morning backwards and forwards to the fountain. Today was her family's turn to thresh their wheat.

'Girlie! Go and get more water... this is like piss!' the men would shout. So, once again, she would have to set off on the long walk to the fountain, carrying as many flasks as she could manage. She was the 'water carrier' – this was her task. Everyone else was busy doing their own jobs.

The work was hot and dusty, and her mother and father were sweaty and covered in chaff and dust. They had to work hard. Her father's job was to keep the machine fed with bundles of wheat, while her mother filled the sacks as the wheat came out at the other end. The whole family helped on such occasions. Zio Domenico threw the bundles to her father using an extra long pitchfork, while Zio Luigi and his sons collected the bales of straw and stacked them up.

The owner of the threshing machine was a travelling man who went around all the villages during the wheat season. His job was to make sure that the motor kept working, adding water and oil as needed, and unblocking any straw that got jammed. It was an important job because time was money and he made sure the thresher worked smoothly and this allowed the workers to follow a strict timetable.

On and on they worked, everyone talking and laughing and shouting to be heard above the roar of the machine's engines. Late in the morning, everyone quietened down as they grew tired and had to save their energy. Every so often the owner of the machine would shout and blaspheme as things weren't running smoothly – this was because everyone was exhausted with the heat, and irritated by the dust which got everywhere, up their noses and in their eyes.

Serafina's mother had covered her head and face to keep the chaff out of her hair, but she could not cover her eyes which were now stinging and watering. She kept looking at the sun to see if it was midday and time to stop.

Once their portion of wheat was done the girl's father Raffaele climbed down from the top of the thresher as the travelling man switched off the engine. The girl thought how nice it was to return to the silence of the mountains. Her mother and father counted the sacks of wheat and they seemed happy – there would be enough for bread and pasta for the whole year.

As water carrier, it was Serafina's job to put all the unwanted drinking water into a large blue basin, where the men could wash their hands and faces. It was now time for the midday meal, and Domenico's eldest daughter Concetta and Serafina's nonna arrived, each carrying a basket full of food on their head. Everyone was hungry and sat waiting patiently while the girl's mother Maria helped her mother and niece set out the food. Under the shade of a nearby tree, a cloth was placed on the ground along with plates, forks, glasses and a flask of wine. Then came the food. Concetta cut great slices of fresh bread and flung them onto the cloth. Serafina's nonna then ladled out heaped plates of pasta '*la Zita*' (which were bought especially for this occasion) and added a rich meat sauce with lots of *pecorino* cheese on top. The men each had two servings, followed by sausages cooked in *sugo*, and large chunks of well-matured cheese with the crusty bread. This was all washed down with lots of water and wine – but not too much wine as there was still much work to be done.

After the meal, the men found a shaded spot next to the stacks of straw where they lay down, pulled their hats over their eyes and slept. Sleep came easily to their tired bodies and they slept for at least an hour, through the hottest part of the day. Before long, the engine was restarted and everyone took up their positions; the wheat that belonged to Zio Domenico was now being threshed. Concetta took Maria's place, filling the sacks with wheat. Maria and her mother packed up their things and walked home with Serafina. Rita now took over as the water carrier.

CHAPTER 15
L' Arca

WHEAT WAS A precious thing, it had to be carefully stored, safe from mice and ants and other infestations. It was not stored in the storeroom, it was stored in the kitchen to keep it extra safe.

In the kitchen there were only three pieces of furniture, and two of these were dedicated to the preservation of wheat. In the corner of the room there was *l'arca*, a large box made of wood with a tight lid at the top. At the bottom was a small square hole with a sliding cover. *L'arca* was about two metres square and almost ceiling-height. Another piece, this time called *la massa*, was also made of wood, it was in two parts, the top half like a trough with a lid at the top that opened upwards, and in this was stored great big brown loaves of bread, enough for a week. At the bottom there was storage for other foodstuffs. Then, of course, there was a table and chairs, where the family gathered to eat.

The wheat had been harvested and was ready to be stored, but first what was left of last year's wheat had to be removed and the container cleaned.

The girl's mother was busy doing this; she opened the little hatch and wheat would come flooding out, but at some point the grain would stop flowing and then Serafina would climb the ladder with her mother and she would be lowered into the container so that she could push the wheat towards the hatch.

Now her mother had gone out and the ladder was there up against *l'arca*. Serafina climbed up the ladder to look in the container. Then she thought, 'I will just climb in,' lowering herself in ready for when she had to do her part of the job. She put her legs over the edge, held on with her hands and then let go. Her feet hit the grain but instead of finding a firm foothold, they sank into the wheat and she found herself waist-deep in the golden grain. She was scared. She shouted for her mother. 'Mamma, Mamma!' she cried but her mother did not hear her. She was chatting with friends in the street.

Serafina was finding it difficult to breathe, the wheat now pressing on her chest. Every time she moved she went a little deeper. Just then the thought came to her that if she went any deeper she might die.

She started to panic and struggle, shouting and crying. Then her feet touched the bottom, she could sink no further. A great sense of relief overcame her. She would be alright, all she had to do was wait for someone to come home. But Maria and her friend had made themselves comfortable sitting on a low wall, other people passing by stopped to chat too. There was no hurry, everyone had time, chores could wait – if not done today, done tomorrow.

The one thing that had to be done on time was getting food on the table, the family would return famished at meal times. The women left it to the last minute but then they had to return home, either to eat or to make the meal. So Maria went back inside and put the water on to boil for the pasta. The beans had been simmering beside the fire since early morning. She quickly prepared a salad and busied herself to get the dinner on the table.

Then, one by one, everyone came home ready to eat, everyone that is except Serafina; the plates of hot *pasta e fagioli* were on the table, everyone sat down to eat.

And still no Serafina.

Everyone finished.

And still the child had not returned.

This was most unusual because Serafina was always hungry and never late for her meal.

Maybe she had stayed over at Rita's house and had dinner there.

Dishes all washed and put away. Maria told her son to go and look for his sister. He returned after a while: no, she had not stayed at her uncle's house for dinner. Yes, he had looked for her, he could not find her.

At this point the family were getting a little worried, but not too much. Where could she be?

The girl's nonna was in and out of the house looking for her granddaughter. 'Don't worry, Mamma, she will turn up soon, go and have your nap,' Maria told her mother.

'No, it will be no good to lie down, I won't be able to rest until she comes home,' answered the old woman. 'I will help you clean *l'arca*, you go up the ladder and push the wheat with a brush, I will hold the sack at the bottom.'

Maria climbed the ladder and when she was able to look in she screamed with shock.

'SERAFINA!' she called.

Serafina opened her eyes, she had fallen into an exhausted sleep while the family gathered and ate. Maria laughed with relief that she had found her daughter, it was funny to see her neck deep in the wheat store.

Serafina howled. 'It's not funny, I shouted for you, I called and called, you did not come!'

'Who said that you could go in there without me being with you?' her mother said. 'Stay put, I will call your dad to get you out.'

'Stay put!' exclaimed Serafina. 'As if I could do anything else!'

Serafina cried. She could hear everyone laughing as she struggled to free herself of the tight embrace of the wheat.

After she was released the girl got a good telling off from her mother and father, warning her how dangerous it was to get into *l'arca* without someone else being there and not ever to do it again.

'No fear,' she cried. 'I will never get in there again,' and she never did.

CHAPTER 16

Canneto

IT WAS STILL summertime and the 18th of August was the highlight of the year, one of the great events of the village. Fontitune was the last village before the high mountains and from there you could follow an age-old pass which would bring you to a beautiful deep valley where a river made its way down to the plains.

Deep in this valley, beside the river, there was a sanctuary: a high cathedral which housed the *Madonna di Canneto*. She would rest quietly in the deep peace of the valley for most of the year. But in August many people went there to visit her.

The only way to get to it was on foot. There were many different paths and tracks, but the one passing through Fontitune was one of the best. People came from far and wide to make the pilgrimage.

The girl would watch the people walking by from the *terrazza* (now with a bannister). From there she could see the drinking fountain and many people stopped to take a drink and refill their flasks with the sweet, fresh water (actually, the water they were drinking came from Canneto). Many people were walking with bare feet. The girl was astonished by this as the road in the village and the paths were very rough.

She asked her nonna why they had no shoes on and her nonna explained to her: some people that were not well, or had family who had some kind of sickness or perhaps were dying, would pray for a miracle, and it was traditional to say to the Madonna, 'Please do this for me and I will walk barefoot to Canneto.'

'You know, Serafina, some people have walked barefoot from very far away,' her nonna said. So when the girl saw someone walking with no shoes, she felt sad, and thought if it was her nonna or anyone of her family, she too would have walked barefoot to Canneto. But to most people it was a holiday and there was a lot of singing and dancing en route.

Anyway, for days before the 18th there had been preparation at home: fresh bread made and also a big batch of biscuits and a huge *panettone*. It was one of the few times that sweet treats were baked. The smell in the house was mouth-watering. The biscuits and cake and wine were placed on a table on the *terrazza* with a cloth thrown over; it was thought very rude not to offer hospitality to the passing people. Most would say thank you but they had just eaten, and walk on. But if it was some distant relative that they had not seen since last year, or friends from the other villages (sometimes it would have been people that her dad knew from down in their winter homes), then they would stop and have wine, and biscuits to dip in their wine.

The thoroughfare would be busy with pilgrims for seven days, from the 15th to the 22nd of August. But the day that most of the people in the village would go was the 18th.

Serafina, her mother, her father (who was lucky to be at home that day) and her brother Fortunato set off early in the morning to make the four-hour trek to the sanctuary; her nonna and Vincenzo were left behind. Her mother carried a basket of food on her head; Dad a rucksack with wine and large loaf of bread, and Serafina and Fortunato each with a bag.

There were many people on the path: family groups, children running ahead, engaged couples usually walking on their own, *a fare l'amore*. Sometimes there would be an outburst of hymn-singing, where everyone would join in and the valley would be filled with the sound of Ave Maria, as other people that were further ahead would pick up the refrain: '*Evviva Maria!*' On the other side of the valley there were other pilgrims making their way there, and they would also sing Ave Maria. It was one of the sounds that the girl would never forget; the valley was filled with the sound of singing.

The walk to Canneto would take three to four hours, sometimes the path would take them uphill, sometimes down. The girl was now walking through a beautiful deep forest, her mother and father walking ahead by themselves, talking quietly. She was larking about with a group of her friends. Then, up ahead, her mother and father stopped, they were holding hands and then her father bent down to kiss her mother on the lips. All the children pointed and laughed, jumping up and down. The girl was mortified with embarrassment. She had seen young people *a fare l'amore* kiss when they thought nobody was looking, but she had never seen old people like her mum and dad kiss on the lips, and where everyone could see them too.

She turned to her pals and shouted, 'What are you laughing at, it is not funny! They can kiss, they are married.'

But she was deeply embarrassed. She walked on ahead to join her parents, to stop them from embarrassing her even more. After a while her father walked with Luigi, his brother-in-law. They were best friends and always sought each other out.

The girl walked with her mother and for once was silent, so silent that her mother noticed.

'You are very quiet, why you are not with your friends?' her mother asked.

'Mum,' said the girl, 'you know when you say to us we have to behave well and not to embarrass you?'

'Yes,' said her mother.

'Well, you just embarrassed me, you and Dad are so old and you were kissing where everyone could see you. That was not nice.'

Maria laughed out loud. 'Yes,' she said, 'I'm sorry if we embarrassed you but that place has special memories for me and your dad and every time we pass it we kiss each other because we love each other. You don't understand now because you are young but you will when you are older.'

The girl looked at her mother; she could see she was deep in thought so she left her to join the other kids. Maria was remembering that day, twelve years ago, when she and Raffaele were on the path to Canneto.

Eventually they reached their destination; they left their picnic in a favourite place where the village people liked to eat and gather. There would always be someone who would watch it, not everyone would visit the Madonna. Most people, however, would cross the rough, wooden bridge over the river (at this point it was very narrow), where they would join the throng of pilgrims and make their way into the church for

Confession, Mass and Communion. The girl was excited because this year she too would keep the Sacraments.

Two hours later, they were making their way back to where they had left their things. Serafina thought on the way that keeping the Sacraments was not much fun after all. By now she was really hungry. Her mother laid down a cloth on the green grassy area and brought out the things in the basket: roast chicken, stuffed peppers, *penne* in tomato sauce, still warm as mother had wrapped them in a woollen blanket, onion and potato omelette, sausage cooked in tomato sauce. A feast; they all stuck in and ate their fill.

The people of Fontitune would gather together after their meal. Someone would bring out the *organetto* (small accordion) and the drinking and dancing would begin – a Tarantella – everyone having fun in their own way. By late afternoon it was time to make the return journey; things were packed away, the food was all eaten and the wine all drunk. In fact, the girl's father was well and truly drunk and was having a quarrel with Zio Luigi (something about someone getting more cheese than they were due).

Her dad was like that; he didn't get drunk often but when he did, he always wanted to fight. Anyway, they all set off for home, her father staggering on the narrow path. This was a bit dangerous because if he fell down the steep rocky side of the mountain, he could hurt himself.

So to help him along, Peppino, who was married to one of Maria's nieces, Restituta, walked beside him on the edge of the path with his arm around her father's shoulders to keep him steady and make sure that he would not fall. Raffaele could not forget his quarrel with Luigi and was going on and on about it, still angry. After a stumble in which Peppino saved him from falling over, in his anger he punched a beech tree, saying that was what he would do to Luigi.

Needless to say, his hand got the worst of his contact with the beech and started to hurt and swell. This sobered her father up and they all got home safe, but so tired because by the time they reached home the moon and the stars had appeared. It had been a long day and it was a day that the girl would never forget, although she would go to Canneto many more times in her lifetime.

CHAPTER 17

Zia Chiarina

ONE DAY THE girl's mother, her nonna and also Nannina, Pierino's sister who had come to help, were busy about the house. Her father was down in the stable.

'Get out of the way, Serafina,' said her mother.

'What are you doing, can I help?' answered the girl.

'No, you are just in the way, go away.'

Serafina was a little hurt and went out of the kitchen, she could hear her father in the stable. She went to see what he was doing. As she walked into the courtyard she stopped to look at the hen who was clucking and scratching; she had tiny little chicks who followed her and pecked where the hen had scratched. She thought how kind a hen is to her babies; she is not chasing her chicks away.

She walked into the storeroom in the stable. She stopped for a fraction of a minute, then ran out again. She went to the fountain and took a drink. 'This is just going to be a horrible day,' she thought. Her father was holding a lamb in between his knees. He had a pointed knife at its throat and was about to kill it.

Now Serafina hated to see it, though she had seen it many times and she did love lamb for *pranzo*.

When she went back to the house, the table was set for a lot of people. She counted the plates: twelve.

On the table there was a large plate of *prosciutto*, a large *pecorino* cheese and sliced sausages.

'Who is coming to eat, Mamma?' she asked.

'Zia Chiarina and her family are coming,' Mamma said.

'Zia Chiarina who lives far away and we have never met?' responded the girl.

'Yes, your father's older sister.'

'Has she any children, Mum?' she asked as she followed her about.

'Of course, you have heard us talk about them. She has three: Giuseppina, the eldest, then Johnny and then Pearl, who's about your age. Now take Vincenzo and come back when it is time to eat.' Just then her father walked in with the skinned lamb in his hands. She grabbed Vincenzo and went out.

When she returned, the kitchen was full. Serafina looked in astonishment at such strange people. They were big and round. They were as white as milk. They had such strange clothes; the woman was wearing such a peculiar hat, a thing she had never seen before.

The girl's father pulled the girl and Vincenzo into the room: 'Say hello to Zia Chiarina, Zio Michele and your cousins.'

The woman saw Serafina and Vincenzo, she gave them a big hug and pinched their cheeks and said: '*Come sono belli!*'

The girl's father told her: 'This is Vincenzo.' She gave him an extra kiss and hug.

'Ah Vincenzo, *come Papa* (like our father), God rest his soul.'

After the girl and her brother had kissed and said hello to everyone, things settled down and Zia Chiarina gave all the children a big bar of chocolate, one each! The girl stared in wonder. Overcome with shyness, she looked at her cousins; they were smiling at her. She looked at her uncle, a strange man with glasses and very strange hair, so black, so flat, so shiny. He looked very old.

They all sat down to eat: a feast! Her mother had made all her favourites: egg *tagliolini* with meatballs in tomato sauce. Delicious roast lamb with crispy roast potatoes from the allotment; a lot of salad from Mamma's *orto*, fresh bread, and in honour of the guests, a delicious sponge cake soaked in homemade liquor and a cream made with eggs, sugar and flour.

After the meal was over, Raffaele's other sister Fiorinda came, and her brother Domenico. Pierino and Nannina's father too. Soon the house was full of people all talking at once. Then they all calmed down and sat round the table; mouths open as they listened to their sister as she talked about her life in *Tinburgo* (Edinburgh) and its many wonders. They looked at her with envy for her luck in life.

The young people all gathered on the *terrazza*, looking in wonder at the way the *inglesi* spoke, laughed and dressed. Soon the big boy and girls were having fun larking about, but the younger children could just look on shyly with their mouths open, staring.

Zia Chiarina and Zio Michele stayed in Picinisco for their holiday. They came to Fontitune often to be with their family while Giuseppina, Johnny and Pearl loved to lark about with the young people of the village. The girls were courted by the young men, to them they were exotic and beautiful. They always brought 'Dairy Milk' chocolate, with strange writing on it. It was so good.

CHAPTER 18

To See and Be Seen

IT WAS HALF-WAY through summer. Already there was the feeling that summer would soon be over for the villagers, and thoughts turned to their winter homes.

It was the 20th of August and Picinisco was hosting the last great *festa* of the year, '*La Festa di Santa-Maria*'. Citizens of Picinisco would come from far and wide; it was an event not to be missed. The day was not only a religious celebration, it was also an occasion to see and to be seen, to meet friends and relations, for families to get together before they scattered again all over the country – some even all over the world.

La Festa was also a great occasion for young people. If a young man liked a girl, this was the time to ask her *a fare l'amore* (to ask her out), and if it was more serious, to ask her to marry. The younger girls and boys would parade from one end of the town to the other (*a fare la passeggiata*). They would walk to *il Mondano* (the square) where there was a merry-go-round and see what was going on there, and then walk back to the last bar in town, sit on the wall which overlooked the valley for a while, then walk back again to *il Mondano*, and so it went.

The single girls would walk with their arms linked to their best friend's, talking and laughing, pretending to ignore the boys that followed.

At the girl's household they were ready to set off. Nonna was staying at home; she said she had been to *la festa* many times and the day was too long for her. She would say her prayers from home. Serafina's father was going with them; the shepherds had drawn lots for who could have this day free from work on the mountain, and he had been one of the lucky ones. Mother had her basket ready with food, they were going to make a day of it and return home late at night.

They set off on their four-mile walk to Picinisco, meeting other families on their way and the party atmosphere began to take hold.

Up ahead, Serafina could see Rita walking with her sisters, Concetta and Carmela. She ran to catch up with them; there was also her other cousins, Zio Luigi's daughters Immacolata and Lina, and lots of other girls too.

The girls were happy and in a holiday mood; the seamstress in Picinisco had been busy sewing new outfits for the occasion. They were all dressed in their best, it was a day to see and to be seen, to show off. All the girls had long hair, usually pleated and put up in a bun at the back of the neck, held in place with turtle-shell clasps. The girls that had curly hair were lucky because some hair would escape and curl about their face, adding softness to the otherwise severe style. Some of the younger girls who had lovely extra-long hair would pleat it loosely and leave it to hang at the front over one shoulder. This was considered a little fast because someone would surely pull it. None of the women and girls, even very young girls, would even consider wearing their hair loose.

Serafina and Rita were talking about the clothes that the older girls were wearing, which colour and style they liked and what they would choose when they were grown up. They could not wait.

By this time they had reached the last bend in the road before the town came into view. Serafina and Rita waited while the older girls changed their shoes, which they had carried with them wrapped in brown paper. They took off their stout sandals and put on dainty high-heel shoes, wrapped the sandals in the paper and hid them behind a bush, ready for their return journey home. The girls smoothed their clothes, passed their hands over their hair, bit their lips, pinched their cheeks and they were ready to go. Serafina and Rita giggled together and did the same, imitating the girls.

As they walked towards the convent, on the left side of the road there was a three-storey building, it was the office of the police and forest rangers. The men would stand on the balcony, lean on the rail and wait for the girls from up-by to pass. The girls were considered beautiful and unspoiled; strong, robust girls bursting with health. The young officers would make flattering comments and whistle as the girls passed by.

The girls would look up, flash them a look and walk on. 'Oh, how nice they look in their uniforms,' they said to each other with a sigh and a last look back. Serafina passed the convent, this was a big day for the Sisters too. She walked on and came to the open space known as *il Mondano*, which was orientated on one side towards the town and on the other to the mountains and valleys.

The religious aspect of the day was divided into two parts. In the morning the church was packed with people; the priest would say mass, after which there would be a procession. La *Madonna Santa-Maria* would be taken from the church, carried on the shoulders of strapping men, followed by the priest in his vestments with a row of altar-boys. Next came the children who had made their communion that year, followed by the young women, then the brass band playing all the traditional music to give the procession its festive air, and then everyone else who wanted to follow the Madonna. The saint would be taken to the small chapel in the cemetery and left there for the rest of the day.

The second part of the occasion took place at eight o'clock, just as it was getting dark. People would gather at the cemetery with candles in hand. The statue of the Madonna would be carried back up to Picinisco, following the winding road in a candle-lit procession, singing hymns and reciting the rosary. Once *Santa-Maria* reached the *piazza* she would stop there, the priest would give a sermon and the *Sindaco* (the mayor) would make a speech. Then all eyes turned to the sky as fireworks were set off in a spectacular show. Finally, the blessed virgin would be taken back to her place in the church and that, more or less, was the religious part of the day.

The girl followed her mother and held her hand; the town was crammed, *il Mondano* was packed with people sleeping in the open, pilgrims still making their way to Canneto used Picinisco as their last stop. The roads were busy with stalls selling toys, roasted nuts and great piles of watermelon.

Her mother made her way to Carmela's, and left her basket there. The owner of a *cantina*, Carmela was quite happy to hold the basket as later the family would return to eat and buy drinks there.

The girl followed her mother and other women to the church, her brother Vincenzo was with his dad and Fortunato would not be seen all day, or only at meal times, as he went about with his friends. The church was full. The girl made her communion with her mother. The priest gave a raging sermon that the girl did not understand. One thing the girl did know was that he was telling them that he said mass every Sunday, not only on feast days, and they were all going to hell for missing mass on ordinary days. By this time a lot of people were talking and not listening. Other people who wanted to listen would turn and glare at those who were talking, put a finger to their lips and make a hissing sound to tell them to be quiet.

On their walk to the cemetery, the women would sing in a high-pitched wailing note as they followed the procession. When they got to the cemetery they went to visit their dead, afterwards climbing back up to the *piazza*, by this time ready for their meal.

The families would gather together to eat; Raffaele, like a lot of other men, had not followed the procession, he was in the *cantina* drinking with friends. Maria went to the *cantina* where she had left her basket; her husband was there, looking as if he was having a really good time. She could see from his flushed face that he was already well-oiled. He was drinking with *compare* Gerardo, a great friend who had moved from Fontitune to a nearby village, so they had much to catch up on. Maria took her basket ready to put the food out but her husband stopped her. No; they were going to eat at *compare* Gerardo's house. Gerardo insisted, he would be really offended if they did not go.

Maria did not want to go; she was with her sister Lucrezia, her husband and their children, Ricucio, Serafina and Maria. Lucrezia lived down-by and had come to the *festa* especially to be with her family. Maria wanted to spend it with them but what was she to do? She knew that when Raffaele had been drinking there was no talking to him.

Lucrezia knew this and did not want to make trouble for her sister. 'It's alright,' she said. 'We will eat with Mingo and Luigi, we will see you later.'

The girl looked on, she did not like it when her father was like this. When he was drunk he could be great company, everyone sought him out, but then he could turn, wanting to fight. They did not call him *Rabbia* (rage) for nothing, so the girl, with all her family, joined Gerardo, his wife Filomena and their family on the short walk to their house.

The girl and her brothers played with other children while Zia Filomena cooked dinner. The contents of Maria's basket were added to the table and they all sat round the table to eat. The girl and her mother were both relieved as Raffaele was in good form, not drinking too much but still enjoying himself and in the thick of it with his *compare* Gerardo. Afterwards they all made their way to the cemetery to join the candle-lit procession.

Much later, when the festivities were over, they walked back to their village up-by with an overall feeling of satisfaction; it had been a great day and Raffaele was sober enough to carry the sleeping Vincenzo all the way home.

CHAPTER 19

Going for Firewood and Eating Blackberries

IN THE WILDNESS of the mountains there was always something to eat; in late summer there were blackberries everywhere. At this time the games the children played would stop, as they would be gathering as many as they could.

Some of the children would take them home: their mothers would make jam, or jam tarts, but the girl's mother did not do this because she would have to buy sugar, which she thought was a waste of money. Serafina, therefore, would eat them fresh. For the children, who always craved something sweet, it was a real treat.

One day, the girl, Rita and their friend Carmela were going to the beech forest to gather firewood. They each carried a rope and a dishcloth round their necks. As they went along they came to a spread of blackberries. They were huge, black and ripe; no one had been to pick them.

They soon filled the dishcloth and ate as many as they could. Then Rita said, 'Shall we make jam, we have so many?'

They looked around until they found a rock that was flat on the top. Each of the girls then picked a small, clean, round stone which they used as a mallet and the three girls set to work. They would put a handful of berries on the flat stone and mash them with the mallet. They would continue until the berries were all used up and they had a big juicy heap. Then they spread the berries out, covered them with leaves and left.

They walked on until they came to a point where they could look down the valley. At the bottom they could see a river, a ribbon of blue that flowed from Canneto. Beside the river you could see an oasis of green. The people of Picinisco had allotments of vegetables there and orchards of fruit. To the children, who were all starved of sugar, it was like paradise.

The girls went on, they reached the edge of the forest and they each gathered dead twigs and branches. But first they spread their rope on the ground in a straight line. The wood would go on to it in a perpendicular fashion. When they had gathered as much as they could carry, they tied the bundle up, made a cushion with the berry-stained dishcloth; put the bundle on their heads and made their way home. When they came to where they had made the jam, they stopped, each putting down their wood, they looked among the bushes and scrub, searching for something. Eventually they found what they were looking for. A sloe berry bush. They pulled from the bush two or three thorns. Then they went to the stone with the jam on top, sat down and removed the leaves, shooed away any bugs that were on it and started, very delicately eating the sweet feast, using the thorns of the sloe berry as forks. The sun had dried the berries and they were delicious as jam, extra sweet.

CHAPTER 20

Going to the *Orto*

IN THE SUMMER, the girl's mother spent a lot of time in her *orto* watering the vegetables from a small spring that bubbled up from the ground. Directing the water where she wanted by making small channels, Maria created a dyke to catch it, and then with a bucket took water where she wanted. There was not much water at this time of the year and she made the best of what there was.

The girl loved to go with her mother to the *orto*, she would take her sandals off like Mamma and walk in the cool water, the mud squelching between her toes. The spring was just at the bottom of a bank. On top of the bank there was an old apple tree and its shade was lovely and cool. The *orto* was not very far from their closest village, Valleporcina.

When the girl was tired of helping her mother, she would walk to Valleporcina. Zia Antonet, who was the eldest of her mother's sisters, lived there. She already had a married daughter. She also had five more daughters and one son. The youngest daughter, Rosa, was the same age as the girl.

Her Zia Antonet always made a fuss of her. She would give her a handful of sugar almonds and kiss and hug her, and kiss her again and pinch her cheeks.

She had lovely twinkling blue eyes and was always happy to see any of her family from Fontitune.

On this day, Rosa was not at home. She was working the fields with her sisters. When her *zia* told her, the girl looked up. From that direction you could hear singing. The girls always sang when they worked. Their father worked them hard rather than pay a ploughman. He would tell his five daughters to take a spade and stand in a row. Spade in, push with foot, turn over the brown earth. They were so strong and healthy, his girls, they would sing while they worked. His only son, Salvatore, would stay at home in the shade because the sun gave him a headache.

The girl was outside under the shade of a tree when the door to the balcony above opened and Zia Restituta hobbled out with a stick and sat on a chair. She was Antonet's mother-in-law: she was toothless, wrinkled, bent and wore a cardigan even in the summer.

'*Buongiorno*, Zia Restituta,' the girl said, remembering to be polite to old people.

'What have you come here for?' Restituta cackled. She didn't like to have Antonet's family visit because she was fearful that Antonet would give things away, things that were for her family. 'What are you eating?' she said.

'Sugar almonds, *zia* gave them to me,' the girl answered.

'What? Has she not seven children of her own to give to?' the old woman snapped. The girl did not answer and walked away. She went into the kitchen to say goodbye to her aunt who was making a mountain of eggless *tagliatelle* for the family.

She gave the girl another handful of sugar almonds. 'Put them in your pocket, don't let the old witch see them, keep some for Fortunato and Vincenzo,' she said. Another kiss and hug and off the girl went. The old woman looked from the balcony to make sure she did not have a bag.

'Goodbye, Zia Restituta,' the girl called.

As she walked back to where her mother was working, she was remembering a story that her mother had told Zia Chiarina one day, while they were sitting around the table after a meal.

She was saying how hard her life had been, but now things were better; they had their own flock of sheep, the horse, a pig, three healthy children, a house of their own. She grabbed her sister-in-law's hand when she said this: 'Thanks to you, Chiarina.' Then she said, 'To pack up and leave, and start all over again in a strange land with three children and little money, it will be a hard thing to do'. The girl did not understand. Soon there were tears in her eyes. She picked up the end of her apron to wipe them.

The girl's mother went on to tell of the hardships she had endured. She and her mother had lived with her brother Domenico. Maria's father had died six months before she was born. Domenico was already married; he became the head of the household and Maria and her mother were at the beck and call of his wife, Angelina, who was always either pregnant or had a child at her breast. So Maria and her mother did all the work.

Domenico was kind but his wife ruled the roost; she treated his mother well enough, but when he was not there it was another story. Maria had a hard time as she grew up.

She went on to tell Chiarina that when she was twenty they wanted her to marry Michele: 'You know him, you remember Michele? But I just didn't like him, everything about him put me off. I refused *a fare l'amore* with him but he would not leave me alone. Mingo and Mamma would go on at me that he was a good match, he had a house, he had land, they were well off.'

'I liked Raffaele and he liked me but he was an orphan, he was worse off than me. How would we live without the help of our families? Anyway, whether I wanted to or not, I was getting pushed into the engagement.' One day she said: 'Mamma, send me to help Antonet.' She had just had another baby and was up to her ears in nappies.

'When I arrived, I went to wash the nappies and everything else, I hung them up to dry, went to get firewood, lit the fire, prepared the food for the evening meal, cleaned her house and killed and prepared a chicken to make soup for Antonet so that her milk would come for the child.

'Anyway, I never stopped for one minute. Then Antonet's husband Sabatino came home; he had been on the mountain doing his stint with the flock. I could see that he had been drinking. He shouted at me to get some water because he needed to wash and shave.

'I was tired so I said to him he could do it himself because I was making *la cena* (dinner). My God, it was as if he was a mad dog. He came towards me to hit me. I ran to the door to get away from him. He grabbed me and pulled me toward him and he bit me on the shoulder.

I screamed, which caused him to let go and I ran away, left everything and made my way home to Fontitune.

'When I got home, I told my mother everything that had happened, expecting her to comfort me but instead she told me off for answering back. Just then Angelina walked in the door with a child in her arms and another following. She saw me and said: Oh, you are back, there is the basket of nappies – you will just have time to wash them before it gets dark.'

'At that moment I just wanted to scream; I took the blood-stained apron which I had put on the wound on my arm, threw it on the table and told her to do the nappies herself. I ran outside in a flood of tears, I wanted to get away. I walked along the path towards Canneto. When I reached the point where you can see the Valley of Canneto, where the Madonna is, I prayed: "My lady, please help me."'

'Anyway,' she went on, 'when I ran out of the house, Raffaele had seen me and he had followed me. I was sitting on a rock, praying, crying, when he came to me, put his hand on my shoulder and asked what was wrong. And you know the rest.

'We did not go home for three days. My mother was in despair, looking for me everywhere. When she knew that I was with Raffaele, she made a bundle of my things and sent them to me at Raffaele's house.'

When the girl got back to the *orto*, her mother was just packing up to go home. She had a basket full of *zucchini* and tomatoes. She put this on her head and off they went on the long climb to Fontitune.

'How long have you been married, Mum?' the girl asked.

'This month it will be twelve years, why do you ask?' Mamma answered.

'Oh, nothing,' said the girl. 'Do you want a sugar almond...?'

CHAPTER 21

Eagle (*Arpé*)

THE GIRL WAS on the *terrazza*. She was in a wee world of her own, having a fantastic daydream about a boy she liked, the pictures so clear in her head. He was saying to her that she was the most beautiful girl in the village and he wanted to marry her, he could not wait for her to grow up, that he would wait for her forever. Her mind was deep in her dream, but her feet were deep in wheat. That morning her mother had washed a sackful of wheat, which she had then spread on the washed floor of the *terrazza* to dry in the sun, so that it would be clean and ready to take to the mill.

The girl had to turn the wheat over and over so that it would dry on all sides. She did this by making rows upon rows with her bare feet, first one way then the other. She had to watch that birds did not come to peck at it and also to keep cats away. When it was nearly dry she would sit on the floor and play with the grain, making wheat mountains, then smoothing it out. She would write with her finger on the smooth wheat the boy's name, over and over, and his age. He would wait for her forever, he said, in her dream.

After a while she lay down on her back so that she could see the pictures in her head even more clearly.

Up high in the sky, soft fluffy clouds floated by, her eyes focused on a black spot that floated round and round, then she spotted another spot circling, then another. She jumped up! The black spots were eagles, she knew this. She dashed into the house, grabbed two large pot lids and ran outside. '*Arpé, arpé, arpé!*' she shouted as loud as she could, at the same time banging the two lids together to make as much noise as possible.

Soon other children came out already prepared with lids, or a lid and a stick, or anything that would make a noise. The village came alive, the children shouting '*Arpé, arpé, arpé,*' jumping up and down and running about. The women came out to look up at the sky as the eagles circled in the hot air. Then they went to gather their hens. Each had a basket full of corn, which they would shake, calling to the hens as they threw handfuls of corn on the ground. 'Te-te, te-te, te-te!' they called, shooing the hens into their coops to keep them safe from the circling predators. In the meantime the children would continue to make the racket until the eagles flew back up the mountain where there were no noisy children and more hope of a meal.

CHAPTER 22

Going to a Wedding

ONE MORNING ALL the family was up, when there was a knock at the door. Everyone looked up. It was unusual for anyone to knock. Usually they would walk right in or they would shout from the steps.

Serafina's mother opened up and embraced the girl at the door; it was her niece Elena, the daughter of her sister Antonet from Valleporcina. She had come with her fiancé and also her brother Salvatore. They were dressed in their best and most elegant outfits. It was obvious that it was not a normal visit. So formality was the order of the day.

Elena's fiancé was carrying a basket covered with an embroidered white napkin; inside there were white sugar almonds and also a large spoon. 'Zia,' the young woman said, 'We have come to bring you *confetti*. We are getting married, we would like you to come and celebrate it with us.'

Maria got a china dish, which she had for such occasions, held it out and Elena filled it with sugar almonds. After this, Maria took a little tray, put tiny glasses on it and filled them with an orange-coloured homemade liqueur, which she offered to the guests. Formalities over, everyone relaxed. They did not stay long because they had many other invitations to deliver.

After they were gone, the girl said to her mother, 'Can I come?'

'We'll see,' said her mother.

'Please, please, please! I want to come too!'

All day long she kept asking until instead of a 'we'll see' her mother said: 'Alright then, as long as you will be quiet.'

The girl jumped with joy. 'What shall I wear, Mum?' No answer from her mother. She repeated, 'What will I wear, Mum?' On and on she went, all day.

On the day of the wedding her mother was dressed in her best blue skirt with wide pleats, and a sky-blue blouse with lace around the collar. She wanted to look modern because the groom was from Cassino, and thought of as a city person. She was not wearing her usual headscarf and apron (she had an apron that matched her skirt but she did not put it on). At first she said that she felt naked without these two things, but her husband and Serafina kept saying to her that she looked really nice and that she had lovely hair and that it was a shame to have it always covered.

The girl's father was very smart wearing his usual white shirt, and a jacket with a white hanky in the breast pocket. Now it was time for Serafina to get dressed. She was to wear her Sunday dress, she was so disappointed that she had not got a new dress for the wedding – it kind of spoiled the fun for her, but she was trying to make the best of it. So she was standing all washed and scrubbed in her underskirt, waiting for her mother to fetch her Sunday dress so that she too would be ready to go.

Her mother came clattering down the wooden steps with a white box. She pulled out the girl's beautiful communion dress. Serafina looked at her mother with her mouth open. Elena had asked if she could wear her communion dress because she wanted her to be her little angel and carry her veil. What joy. What happiness! She slipped into its silky softness. Her mother had mended the frill that she had damaged on the day of her First Communion. She put on her gloves, she would not need her little lace bag today, but then again she would take it with her, she could fill it with confetti (the paper kind). And afterwards fill it with real *confetti* (sugar almonds).

She tried to push her feet into her white shoes but her feet must have grown because she could not get them on. So she had to wear her Sunday best, but they were not white, they were a light brown. 'Never mind,' said mother, 'under the long dress you can't see them.' The girl was glad – at least they did not hurt.

It was the custom that all the people who were invited to the wedding would gather at the house of the bride and from there they would walk to Picinisco. It was a long walk. No one in the village had a car, but in Picinisco some people did. The bride's father had hired a car to take the bride to church and also a bus to take guests that did not have transport.

That was all very well, but there was still a lot of walking. The walk down to Valleporcina was two miles alone. There, a breakfast of bread and cheese was provided. There would be loud applause when the groom arrived with his mother and father. His mother would bring the wedding dress so she would dress the bride and the father would bring the 'gold' that he would give to his wife to adorn Elena on her wedding day: earrings, necklace, bracelet. They would set off. The bride with her father at the front, followed by the groom and his mother, and everyone else behind. They would then all walk the two miles up to the crossroads and meet the cars and bus which would take the entire wedding party to Picinisco.

Serafina and her cousin Rita, also in her communion dress, were standing importantly behind the bride. 'Now don't let the veil touch the ground,' Elena said. The girls nodded and reassured her that they would be careful.

Now the girls watched as the bride left the house. Her mother would throw handfuls of sugar almonds mixed with paper confetti over the bride and the rest of the company. The children would scrabble to get as many as they could and fill their pockets. Serafina looked on. 'There you go,' she thought. 'There is always an upside and downside to everything.' If she were not holding the veil she would be with the others scrabbling for *confetti* to get as many as possible and eat sweet deliciousness all week.

Then she had an idea; she told Rita to hold the veil out like a net so maybe they could get some confetti landing in it, and it worked. As soon as one landed in their net they would pop it in their mouths, and some they put in Serafina's lace bag.

Elena looked back and laughed. 'Don't worry, girls, I will give you *confetti* later.' What a relief thought Serafina as they returned to their duty, and kept the veil gliding just above the ground.

When they got to Picinisco, the *piazza* was full of people waiting to greet and admire the bride. The townspeople always found the folk from up-by amusing. 'But if it was not for the people of up-by who had cash to spend, the people of Picinisco would be in a very sorry state,' she had heard her nonna say to one of her friends. So the girl looked to see if they were making fun this time, but everyone looked on admiringly.

Church over and photos taken, off they went to the house of the groom to have the wedding feast. Free from her duty, the girl was running and playing. When the dancing began, the children wanted to dance too, but they kept being pushed out of the way by the adults. So they had their own dance area, away from the dance floor.

It was late when they climbed on the bus ready to go home. While they were passing through Cassino, there was a great mass of people and the bus had to stop. Everyone got out to watch what was going on. The girl's father held her hand tight in case they were separated. All of a sudden Serafina screamed and clung to her father. Through the crowd; there was the tallest man she had ever seen, really tall, twice the height of a normal tall man. He was so scary. Her father and mother laughed at her. The girl did not think it was funny; if he grabbed her and ran away, how would an ordinary person like her dad catch him?

It was years later that the girl understood the man had been on stilts.

CHAPTER 23

All Able-Bodied Men

IT WAS CHILLY now at night. In her sleep the girl pulled the bed covers under her chin and tried to snuggle closer to her grandmother, but as hard as she tried she could not do it... She opened her eyes and realised that her nonna was not there beside her. 'Ah,' she thought. 'That's why I can't get warm. Nonna is not here; she must have gone to the toilet.'

She snuggled down, trying to go back to sleep as it was still dark outside, but sleep would not come. She lay still with her eyes open, waiting for her nonna to come and get back into bed. She waited and waited and thought she would have to get up and see why her nonna was taking so long, and eventually she did. The girl wrapped a blanket around herself and padded out in bare feet.

Nonna was not in the kitchen. She opened the door and walked out on the *terrazza*. She stood and looked with wonder and amazement at the sky. She had never seen it like this. The sky was so black, with so many stars that were so bright, so close, she felt as if she could stretch out her hand and take one.

The girl thought, where could Nonna be? Surely she couldn't be in the toilet all this time. She walked down to the courtyard and called but she was not there. She ran up the steps into the house. Maybe Nonna had stayed over at Zio Luigi's house, sometimes she did that. The thought of going back to bed on her own was frightening; the heavy silence, the dark bright night. She was trying hard not to think of spirits and ghosts. No, she was too scared, she walked up the steps to her mother's room, she would just slip in beside her. She padded quietly over to the bed and stood: her mother and father were not there. She dropped the blanket and ran down the steps, she went to the bed where her two brothers were asleep.

She shook Fortunato awake. 'Where are Mum and Dad? They are not in their room and Nonna is not here either.'

Fortunato got out of bed and put his trousers on, he also checked all over the house just to make sure that what Serafina was saying was true. The girl followed him about, not wanting to be left alone.

Fortunato said, 'Something must have happened.' He would go to Zio Luigi's house and see. 'You stay here with Vincenzo,' he said to the girl.

'No, I'm not staying here on my own,' she said. By this time she was crying. Her brother was looking very worried, which made the girl shiver with fright.

'Go and put your clothes and shoes on,' Fortunato said to her as he stood on the *terrazza* thinking what to do. When the girl came out again he was leaning on the wall, looking down, into the distance. Serafina stood beside him and looked also. In the valley, towards Valleporcina, she could see lights swaying on the road and as they got closer they could hear voices.

When they got to the point where the road would turn to go towards Picinisco, she could see there was a row of stretchers, each being carried by four men. A line of people followed, some saying the *Padre Nostro* prayer; others crying, some wailing. They watched until they disappeared.

'My God, what has happened?' said Fortunato. 'We had best stay here until it gets light, then we will find out,' he told his sister.

Zia Antonet and her family had eaten mushrooms that her husband had picked. They had eaten mushrooms many times before but in this batch there must have been one or two poisonous ones and these had made the whole family very ill.

When the girl's nonna and mother and father had heard, they rushed down to see what they could do. They tried to make them sick by giving them milk mixed with salt. This worked, but they were still not at all well so they took them on stretchers to the doctor in Picinisco, all able-bodied men helping in the effort.

They all recovered. The doctor said that giving them milk and salt and making them sick probably saved their lives.

No more mushrooms for them! The girl's mother would never have them in the house.

CHAPTER 24

The Sheep Return

AUTUMN CAME EARLY in the mountains; the days shorter, the nights cold. Life in the village slowed down; the harvest was in, the grain in storage. The corn was ripe and ready to gather. Everything that was done in the village was done as one large family (today you help me, tomorrow I'll help you). So things were soon finished. There was a stillness now and even the children were subdued. There was a sense of waiting for something and it soon came – the thundering of hoofs as the great flock of sheep were herded down the mountain.

At the top of the village they were penned up, the dogs barking, the children running about shouting. All the men helping, including the boys. Fortunato had helped too, and everyone was covered with dust. Mother went to the boy to give him a flask of cold water to drink and then he cupped his hands and his mother poured water in them so he could wash the dust from his face. The mother looked at her son; he looked tired, he was just a child, she lifted her hand to pass it over his head, resisting the urge to kiss him. Parents were like that. Kiss the child, spoil the child – that was a saying that Serafina had heard many times.

Now, every sheep had his owner's mark on it, some on the rump, some on the shoulder, some in red, others in blue, and so on. This was the time that each owner would reclaim his own herd of sheep with the help of his dogs, wife and children. He would bring them to be penned in the same fields as in springtime. The herd would graze around the village until all the grass was eaten up and then it would be time to make the move again to the plains, down-by, where it was warmer and did not snow in the winter.

Most families would go again and again to the same place as previous years but if they had not gotten on there the year before, they would look for somewhere different. The girl's father Raffaele was always on the lookout for a good place to go for the winter. What made it a good place? It had to be where there were no other shepherds nearby; where he could rent plenty of grazing land for the sheep. Somewhere there was a town nearby where he could sell their *ricotta* and, in spring, their lambs. Also there had to be a school for the children. Some of the children of the village did not go to school in the winter, making do with summer school. Raffaele wanted his children to be educated because he knew what it was like not to be able to read and write. He did not want that for his children.

So it was about this time of the year when he would leave the herd in the hands of his wife and son, and go to Picinisco, where he would hire a car and driver and go to various places, scouting about until he found one that he liked. He would then look for a house where they could spend the winter, which had stables for the animals and accommodation for the family. Once he had agreed a price and left a deposit he would come home.

Now that was what usually happened but this year was different. Raffaele did not take the trip, but was at home. He was always deep in thought, people would speak to him and he would not hear. He would have long talks with Maria. Talking about things that the girl did not understand. Her nonna would listen then walk away with a tear in her eye. The men of the village were in and out of the house talking about sheep, talking about Peppa.

The girl always looked on quietly, trying to understand, but she could not.

One day there was a lot of talk in the house, sometimes silence, other times talking, talking, talking, and again silence.

It was on a day like this that the girl did not go out to play; she was feeling nervous. She was outside on the *terrazza* watching for who might go by. Her father walked out and went into the stable for Peppa. She could hear her mother and nonna inside, talking.

Then Fortunato came out, his eyes bright, he looked happy: 'What's going on?' she asked her brother.

'Why, have you not twigged yet?' he said. 'We are going away.'

'I know we are going away,' she said. In fact, a few of the families had already left for their winter homes.

'Yes, but we are not going down-by, we are going to *la Scozia*, where Zia Chiarina lives.'

Serafina was stunned to hear this – she had an overpowering feeling of fear and excitement. She ran into the house to ask her mother. When she walked into the kitchen her mother and grandmother were sitting close together, holding each other's hands, both crying.

Serafina ran to her nonna, who embraced her. She looked at her mother. 'Is it true what Fortunato said, that we are going to live where Zia Chiarina lives?' she asked.

'Yes,' said her mother.

'And why are you and Nonna crying, don't you want to go?' she asked. It did not enter her mind to ask why they were moving so far because all things were decided without consideration of what the children thought.

'Yes, I want to go, me and your father have talked it over and we think it will be a better life for you, Fortunato and Vincenzo,' her mother said.

'Then why are you both crying, Nonna, are you not happy to go?'

Her mother looked at her. 'Nonna won't be coming, dear, she will stay with Zio Domenico and Zio Luigi.'

Serafina felt a huge shock of emotion, she clung to her nonna, an overwhelming feeling of panic overcame her and in a flood of tears she pressed her face into her grandmother's chest and cried: 'I'm not going if Nonna doesn't come too!'

Her mother tried to soothe her but she would not be comforted, she just clung to her nonna and sobbed, drinking in her softness, her smell, her warmth.

The girl's mother went out of the house; she could not bear to see her mother and daughter distraught. Their grief made her question whether they were doing the right thing.

Maria saw her husband go out with Peppa, harnessed; he was going for firewood. 'Wait, I'm coming with you,' she called to him as she quickly changed her sandals for stout boots. They walked up through the village, taking the path to Canneto to go to the beech forest where there were plenty of dead logs and branches littering the forest floor so they would soon have a load for Peppa.

As they walked on the narrow path side by side, with the horse on a lead following, they were talking about Raffaele's going away soon, and if they were they doing the right thing. She was telling him how upset her mother and daughter were to part.

Soon they were at the point where they could see the Valley of Canneto. They looked at each other, and he said, 'Are you remembering?'

'How can I forget?' she said. He took her in his arms and kissed her. She clung to him. 'I can't bear being parted from you. I can't live without you,' she said.

'As soon as I have somewhere for us to live, I will send for you because I can't bear to be away from you either,' he answered. He tied the horse to a tree. He stretched his hand out to her, she took it. He led her to a hidden place, sat down and pulled her to him. After, as she lay in the crook of his arm, he fell asleep and she was remembering that day, twelve years ago, when she ran away and he followed.

She had felt his hand on her shoulder before she saw him. 'What's wrong?' he said, 'Why are you crying?' Her eyes overflowed with hot tears, he pulled her towards him and enfolded her in his arms and let her sob, stroking her back and murmuring comforting words. When she could, she pulled away from him but all she wanted to do was to stay in his arms forever. She stood up and walked away to put some distance between them. She sat on a bank soft with moss.

'I don't know what to do,' she said. 'I am a slave to my family, Angelina can't bear to see me sitting down, always finding things for me to do. Mamma says to keep quiet, keep the peace. It will get better, but when? I just can't take it anymore,' and she went on to tell him what had happened that day, showing him the bite on her arm.

Raffaele walked over to her to look at the bite and as he looked his eyes darkened with anger. He lifted her arm to take a better look. 'He will pay for this,' he said. 'He is a mad dog. Look at the wound, it's swollen and red. I hope it doesn't get infected.' Then, on impulse, he bent down to kiss her arm. 'There, I will kiss it better for you,' he said with a smile.

She looked into his eyes, her face flushed hot, her heart beating, the touch of his lips on her skin, the scrape of his stubble was a sensation so sweet that it made her cry with longing. She wanted to drown in his eyes. With great effort she pulled her gaze away and looked into the distance, towards Canneto. She could almost hear '*la Madonna*' tell her to get up and go home. But her legs would just not move. Her eyes were drawn to his, she had no control of them. Their eyes met, the message clear in both their looks.

Raffaele dropped her hand and walked away, trembling, trying to resist the impulse to take her in his arms, to kiss her burning lips. 'I can't do this to her,' he thought. 'I can't marry her, I will ruin her, I will make her suffer,' and he could not bear that. Maria watched him walk away and knew she should be doing the same, but no matter how much she told her legs to move, she still couldn't, she sat there and watched him.

He stopped, he sat on a rock facing Canneto with his back to her, his head down, then he put his hand to his face. His shoulders were shaking; he was sobbing, crying as if his heart would break.

At that moment her legs had a will of their own, she sprang up, she threw all care away and ran to him, she put her arms round him, pressed her face to his back: 'Don't cry, my darling.' But she was crying too, great sobs into his back. He turned round, stood up to embrace her, their lips met and they were lost. She melted into him, her body was liquid, she felt that she could not stay standing but must lie down, her legs were no longer her own.

He held her up, holding her close, so close that if she went down there would be no turning back. He pushed her to a nearby tree so that she would not fall and there he kissed her, pressing his body to her to receive an answer. He wanted to stop kissing her but his lips would not obey him. Maria was feeling the sweet pressure of his lips, her lips were swelling, his beard scratching her lips and face. This made her come to her senses. How could she go home in such a state! She put a gentle pressure on his chest to push him away.

'No,' she said, 'we must not.' Her words were so right, he pulled away from her.

'Yes,' he said, 'we must not.' He walked away from her. How could they marry? He had nothing to live on.

The war had ruined the villagers, what they had was all gone. The Nazis, *che gli possa sta al'infern* had taken all their livestock and cleared their homes of any food. They even took down the doors to use as firewood. When the war was over and the villagers went back to their homes.

They had to start from scratch. That had been only three years ago. He walked back to Maria, still leaning on the trunk of the tree, her hands behind her back.

'What shall we do?' he said to her.

By this time it was dark but there was a full moon, a beautiful August night, the air warm and scented with the wild flowers and herbs of the mountain.

'It is late, you must go home,' he said, but his voice, his eyes, his body said please stay, don't leave me.

'Yes, I must,' she answered but made no move to do so. Raffaele stood and looked at her, his heart pounding in his chest. She looked back at him, her lips parted, her heart in her mouth – she could not breathe. He stretched out his hand to her, she took it and he led her into the forest.

'What shall we do now?' he said to her as she lay in the crook of his arm.

'Whatever you say, as long as I am with you.' With her hand, she was feeling his face, his eyes, his nose, his mouth, his hair. Every part of him was now part of her. At last she was no longer alone, at last there was someone to love her, a love that was just for her, to share her life, her body, her everything.

'My darling,' she said, 'as long as we are together, you are mine and I'm yours. We will face whatever comes.'

'Yes,' he said. He was feeling the same, at last he was not alone but could lie every night with Maria by his side. What happiness! They were one.

They slept in each other's arms, their bodies entwined. The chirping of birds woke them to the reality of their new life, they would wake every morning now like this. They kissed with hot passion.

After, she said to him, 'Shall we walk to Canneto?'
They walked hand in hand, mostly in silence. Their
happiness was too precious to spoil with words. When
they got to the church, it was closed; it had not been
used since the war but it did not matter. They stood
before it and made their vows to each other in the deep
stillness of the valley and their hearts were at peace.

He told her to wait there for him, he knew
somewhere he could get some food. 'No, don't leave
me,' she said. To part with him was like ripping a
part of her away.

He laughed at her and said: 'You must be hungry
and so am I. I won't be long.'

She sat and prayed, 'Oh my God, forgive me if I
have done wrong.' But within herself she was not
sorry, she had no regrets.

After a while Raffaele came back with a sack full
of fruit and vegetables. He had raided the allotments
by the river that belonged to the people of Picinisco.
They stayed out for three nights, eating the fruits of
the forest and drinking the sweet water of Canneto.

Then it was time to go back home and face their
families and neighbours. A week later they went to
Picinisco and got married.

CHAPTER 25

It Was Like a Highway

THE CHILDREN WERE always on the lookout for entertainment. It could be anything and nothing: a dead snake, fighting dogs, fighting people, someone drunk going home and his wife shouting at him. The children were spectators of everything. There was a lot of teasing. There could sometimes be cruelty, tears too, but the beauty of it was that it would pass. Next day, friends again. It was up to the children, parents did not get involved, and because it would not be pondered over, it was of the moment. You were what you were, you did what you did; as long as there was no blood, all was well. This applied even more to older children, children of the girl's age were all still innocent – in the outer circle looking on with big eyes, taking it all in.

Fontitune was a sleepy village on the side of a mountain but sometimes it felt like a highway. If they wanted to go to the high mountains, people from Picinisco would pass through it. Woodcutters would pass through with their mules, groups of women would pass in the morning, returning late in the day with sacks full of mountain herbs on their heads, which they would sell at the Atina market. In the autumn they would go to gather snails, big white ones, then it would be mushrooms. For these women, the money they earned this way would be the only cash they would see.

One time, an old, grey bent man came into the village. By the time he reached the girl's house he already had a tail of children following him. He shouted from the bottom of the steps, 'Missus, come and see, help an old man to live!' He had on a pole the dried-up body of a fox. 'See,' he said, 'one less pest to eat your chickens.' The girl's mother was not at home so her nonna came out to have a look. Nonna looked at the fox and laughed.

'Hey, old man, that fox looks like the same one as last year,' she said. The old man opened his mouth to reveal his toothless gums and laughed too.

'Hey Missus,' he said, 'with this great misery, who has the strength to chase foxes?'

The girl's nonna went into the house and reappeared at the door asking the man if he had eaten, was he hungry

'I am always hungry, Missus,' he answered, 'and so are the ones at home. What can you do, with this great misery?'

The grandmother came out, in her apron she carried six eggs, a chunk of bread and a small round cheese. She put the eggs in the man's basket, and also the bread and cheese.

The man said: '*Per l'anima dei tui morti*' (may God reward your dead for your good deed). Serafina joined the other children as the man made his way through the village.

Sometimes a man would come to sharpen knives and axes, anything that needed sharpening in fact.

He would sit on his contraption and treadle away with his feet, like he was working a sewing machine. The children would watch as the sparks came off his grinding stone. Again, he would receive payment in kind, very rarely money.

One very hot afternoon, the girl was on the *terrazza*. She could hear a crowd of children coming down the road. 'It's Gughiermo,' they were shouting. The girl went to the gate to see what there was to see. This man, Gughiermo, was bounding down the road, behind him his mule loaded with wood. Gughiermo had gone to the forest to get firewood for his family. He was going home but he was going at such a rate he was almost running. His eyes red and bloodshot, he looked like a madman. The children knew what was coming next; they had seen this before.

As soon as he got to the fountain he let go of his mule and put his head and as much of his body as he could under the fountain. He would splutter and groan, come out from under the water and shake himself like a dog. He would do this again and again, sometimes he would shout to the children and chase them away.

The children would laugh and scatter and regroup to peer at him. Eventually Gughiermo would calm down, sit and rest. He would refill his flask of water, take a last cooling dip, take his mule and go home. The children all went their own way. The show was over for today. The girl walked up to her house. Her mother was on the *terrazza*, she had been watching Gughiermo as well. Serafina's mother looked sad. The girl asked her mother why she was not laughing. Her mother explained to her that it is not nice to laugh at people. Gughiermo had a problem and could do nothing about it. 'What's wrong with him?' Serafina asked.

Her mother explained: 'He has a disease, he does not sweat like you and I so when he gets hot, he gets really hot. To find some relief he has to do what he does.'

One man that the children really liked when he came to the village was the scrap metal man. He did not come often because there really was not much trade for him. Metal was rarely for scrap. The reason the girl and the rest of the children enjoyed his visits was that as soon as it was known he was in the village, the children would scamper home and beg for any old scrap, a fork or a spoon, an old pot, a lid, anything at all. The children would take this to the scrap man and he would give them a small toy, a whistle or a mouth harmonium. One time he gave all the children bubblegum, a thing the children had never seen before. They chewed like crazy, blowing bubbles all day long. But these days were rare. Most of the time, in the village there were just the villagers.

CHAPTER 26

Dad Leaving

THE GIRL WATCHED and listened to everything that was happening. She could kick herself for not understanding what was going on before, but now that she knew what they were talking about, everything was much clearer.

Her father had sold his sheep, that was why he was at home so much. The other shepherds of the village had shared the herd between them. They had also taken the dogs so Serafina did not go to feed them anymore. Caponero still came to the house, though, and sought out his master wherever he was, often sitting at the bottom of the steps. Serafina would pet him and sit beside him. She had been told not to feed him, so he would go back to his work with the sheep, but he was confused. Where was his herd and who was his master?

Raffaele would take his horse Peppa, put her harness on and go to the beech forest to gather firewood. He would do this most days. He would stack the wood under the *terrazza*. He already had his train ticket for the journey to Scotland. He would go first and his family would follow later. Maria and the children would spend the winter in the village; when the snow came it would be very cold. He was getting as much wood as he could so that they would be warm.

The families of the *paese* were also getting ready to go, not to Scotland but down from the mountain. They packed the things they would need for the winter. Every day someone would come to the house to say goodbye but it was not the goodbye of before when Raffaele's brother and sisters and their families would pop in, shake hands, give a pat on the back and a cheerfully say, 'Take care, have a good winter, see you in spring. If you have any trouble, let me know. Good luck! Make lots of money!'

No, they came with a tear already in their eyes, their faces glum. They would embrace and cry: 'Goodbye brother, look after yourself, God willing we will see each other again.'

'Goodbye sister, *ti voglio bene*, I love you. Take care of yourself, hope all goes well when the baby comes.' Raffaele was the youngest of his family, the young uncle. He had grown up playing with his nieces and nephews, so they loved him. Some of them were inconsolable and sobbed. Serafina would cry too.

There was a special boy, Ernesto, Raffaele's brother's oldest child. He was small for his age, he was not very strong, but he had been doing the work of a man for years, his father not taking into account his weakness. He would often be barefoot, and Raffaele would make him a pair of *cioce*: rough leather sandals with straps that wound round the lower leg to keep them on.

Ernesto's father was often drunk, he would not do what had to be done and would send the boy to do a man's work. When they were out with the herd on the hillsides, Raffaele would share his food with him, sometimes going without himself to give to the boy. And when it was cold, he would take the boy on his knee and hold him close, wrapping the great black felt cloak around them both to keep warm.

Serafina was on the *terrazza* watching people come and go. Her father was leaving: next day, in the early morning Middiuccio, the taxi man, was coming to pick him up at the bottom of the village. Zio Luigi was going with him as far as Rome where he was to take his train.

From the *terrazza* the girl was watching her cousin Ernesto, who was sitting at the bottom of the steps. Sometimes he would make a dash, as if to go home. Then he would come back and sit again. He would look up. He reminded Serafina of the dog, Caponero – the same look of sadness and loss.

The stream of people finished and Ernesto was still at the bottom of the steps. 'Come up,' called the girl. The boy was crying as he came up. He walked into the house, he embraced his uncle. The girl's father was crying too.

'I will send for you, once we are settled, when you are eighteen.' He went into the back room and came out with his black cape. 'Here,' he said. 'It will keep you warm, and think of me when you wear it.'

The boy clasped the cloak and ran out. 'Goodbye, Zio. I will not forget you, please don't forget me.'

It was still dark. Serafina was woken by her nonna getting up. 'It's early, go back to sleep,' she said, but Serafina could not go back to sleep, not without her nonna's warm body to curl up against.

Her nonna lit the fire, put the *cioccolatiera* (a kind of tea pot) full of water next to the embers to make tea.

After a while the hatch opened and her mother and father came down. His case was full and a satchel with food enough for the three-day journey. He was ready.

'Go and wake up Fortunato, but be careful and don't wake Vincenzo,' her mother said to Serafina. Vincenzo would howl if he saw his father go. Zio Luigi arrived. He said that Middiuccio was here, he had seen the light of his car.

Raffaele was ready to go. Everyone would walk with him to the bottom but he had to say goodbye to Mamma, there in the house. He embraced her, both of them in tears.

'Look after yourself, thank you so much for everything you have done for us. If I have ever shown disrespect for you, I'm sorry. *Ti voglio bene.* I love you. I'm not going away forever. I will come back.'

'God go with you, don't leave it too long before you send for Maria – families should be together,' answered the girl's nonna. Everyone was crying. It felt as if it *was* forever. The girl sobbed, thinking of when she would have to leave her nonna.

CHAPTER 27

Going for Wine

THE EATING OF bread and cheese and the drinking of wine were the mainstays of the girl's family meals. Even the children would drink some wine at the table.

The bread and cheese were easy, they grew their own wheat and made their own cheese. Wine was one of the things they did not have so it had to be bought from down-by, in the plains of Picinisco. Even so, the girl's mother figured a way to produce her own wine and spend as little as possible.

One morning, the girl's mother was getting ready to go to Picinisco. She was putting the harness on Peppa. The girl thought that maybe she was going to the water mill again and asked if she could go with her.

Her mother said yes, but only if she would hurry, wash and change into clean clothes. The girl ran to do this. When she got back and was ready to go, her mother had loaded two wooden barrels on Peppa. They were not going to the mill after all.

'Where are we going, Mum?' she asked.

'We are going to get wine.'

'Where is that, Mum?'

'Down-by,' said her mother.

'How long are we going away for, Mum?'

'All day,' her mother answered.

And so on: questions and answers, all the way. Maria thought Serafina must be the most inquisitive child in the world.

When they got to the cemetery, instead of turning at the road to go down to the mill, they kept on walking. Although it was called the plains, it was not really flat plains but rolling hills. They passed little farmsteads, little groups of houses, and on the way the girl's mother would talk to whoever she met.

When they came to a little hamlet, they had reached their destination. The girl thought that they would fill their barrels with wine and go home, but that was not how it was to be.

Maria was speaking to an old man. He was unwashed and smelly, he had a grey beard and was toothless but he laughed a lot and was nice. Maria and the man set to some gentle haggling. When a price was agreed they each picked up some wooden boxes and some baskets and walked away. The girl followed, her mother telling her, 'You bring a basket too, Serafina.'

When they got to the vineyard there were row upon row of grapes: big yellow bunches. The girl looked on greedily. Her mother and the man put the boxes down and started to pick the grapes to fill the boxes. 'You help too, Serafina,' said her mother, giving her a small knife to cut the grapes from the vines.

Serafina wanted to eat some. She went to her mother and whispered in her ear, 'Can I eat some, Mum?'

Her mother laughed and said to the man, 'She asked if she can eat some.'

He laughed too and said, 'Eat as much as you want.' And she did.

When the boxes were full, Maria would put a box on her head, a basket in each hand and take it back to the old man's farmstead. She had to do quite a few journeys before they had enough.

'I think that these will do,' said the man. He put a box on his shoulder. Serafina carried a basketful and her mother also carried as much as she could.

At the farmstead all the grapes were ready to be turned into wine. Serafina was curious to see how this miracle would happen.

In a barn the man had a big barrel with a metal post in the middle and over the barrel a wooden box with a wheel. He would throw the grapes in the box and Maria would turn a handle on the wheel. The grapes would be crushed and fall in. This was heavy work. Maria was very hot and sweaty while the girl sat in the shade eating endless grapes. When all the grapes were crushed the box was taken off, wooden blocks were placed over the top, followed by a heavy weight attached to a pole. Her mother and the man pushed and pulled on the pole and as the weight descended a white sticky juice came pouring out from a spout at the bottom. They filled the barrels they had brought with the sweet liquor.

The girl's mother and the man kept pushing and pulling on the pole until the press ran dry and their barrels were full. All was done; the girl's mother washed her hands and face, and the girl did the same.

The farmer's wife asked them to rest and stay for

something to eat. It would not take long to prepare some sausage and *prosciutto*. She said this at least three times to show she meant it and it was no trouble, but the girl's mother said no, it was too late and they must get home; also it looked as if it was going to rain so they'd better make a start, and off they went.

As they started their homeward journey, the girl's tummy started to rumble and boil. 'Mum, my tummy's sore,' she said. 'Mum, I think I need to go.'

'Then go behind that bush,' her mum said. Serafina went.

'Mum, I need to go again!'

'Go behind that tree,' she said.

'Mum, my tummy is really sore.' This time Maria went with her to hold her hand. When Serafina got up, her mother looked and laughed: grapes, some still whole.

'How many grapes did you eat, you greedy thing?' asked her mother.

'Well, the man said I could eat as many as I wanted.'

'Come on,' said her mother, 'I think it is going to rain. Let's walk to that house up ahead – if it rains we will shelter there'. And sure enough, a downpour came. The woman at the house said to put the horse in the barn and come in for something to eat, and so they did.

When they got home, they poured the wine into great big glass containers that were covered with straw and these were left under the wooden steps in the back room. And there, the heady smell and gentle seething of the fermenting wine would put Nonna, the girl and her brother to sleep.

CHAPTER 28

All Souls' Day

AFTER THE GIRL's father left to go to a town called *Tinburgo* in *la Scozia*, one by one the other families left too. In the village there were only a few people and most of the children had gone. Of Serafina's playmates, only Rita was left. She had stayed behind with her brother Narduccio and his young wife. They were to stay until it was time to kill the pig. This applied to most families, someone would be left behind to look after the pig until it was time for slaughter. The weather had to be right: cold and all the flies gone.

The girl's mother was busy; the thought of spending the winter in Fontitune without her husband was frightening. She filled her day with things she had to do to make the winter comfortable for her mother and children.

Most of the vegetables that she had produced from her *orto* were either pickled in vinegar or *sott'olio* (in oil). She had picked the apples from the tree in her *orto*; they were stored on a deep bed of straw, with another thick blanket of straw on top. They would last all winter, to be eaten raw or cooked. All of the bad apples, which couldn't be eaten, she fed to the pig.

Normally at this time of the year she would be cleaning out the stables and bringing the manure to her fields and especially to her *orto*, so that next year she would have a bumper crop. Only this year she did not do this because she would not be here.

Even just the thought of being away from Raffaele for so long would give her long sleepless nights.

In the morning Maria would give each of the children a small sack and tell them to go and gather chestnuts. The children knew where the best were, they walked down through the village to the bottom. They passed the last house on the way to a place known as '*La Madonnina*'. On an alcove at the foot of a large chestnut tree was a little statue of *la Madonna*. There, the children made the sign of the cross and began their foraging. They looked for nuts under the leaves, some still in their spiky casing. With two sticks they pulled the case apart and ate the fruit. This was why this tree was everyone's favourite: you could eat the fruit raw! Simply crack open the outer shell, pull the brown pith from the yellow flesh and crunch away.

With only a handful to be found the children walked on. They left the road and followed a path uphill through a wood until they came to a clearing: this was where most of the chestnut trees were.

From here you could see the village, it was facing them. The beech forest was turning red. The tops of the mountain were snow-covered. They rummaged in the leaf litter, the nuts were hidden there, because the trees were shedding their leaves. The nuts would not fall all at once, so if they returned over two or three days they would always find some. It was some time before they filled their little sacks, because they had to share with other people and animals who also sought out these forest delights.

The girl's mother wanted as many as they could find because when the days were short and the nights long, they would sit by the open fire and roast the chestnuts or put them in a clay *pignatta* (pot) filled with water, push it into the embers and let it simmer away. Serafina liked them best this way. Bite into a soft nut and squeeze its hot fleshy deliciousness into your mouth.

The people of Fontitune, or what was left of them at this time of year, would gather together at night and sit by the fire in one house or the other.

Sometimes they would bring out a great basket of corn to remove the outer leaves. They would take up a pile, put it on their laps and chat away while their hands were busy revealing great, golden cobs of ripe corn.

The girl liked it best of all when they would tell stories. She would sit next to her nonna so that she could hold on to her if she was frightened. It was coming up to the *festa di tutti i morti*, when the dead would be remembered.

The stories round the fire would be of people who had passed away. How they had lived and died. There would be stories of spirits that had appeared and spirits that would come in dreams. There were ghosts that appeared in certain parts of the village because something horrible had happened there. Great white dogs that would cross your path and then disappear. There were other spirits who would entice you to follow them until you were hopelessly lost.

The girl sat on a stool between her mother and her grandmother. She pushed herself as close as possible to the fire, her knees were burning but she would not pull back, she wanted to have someone behind her because once they started to tell stories, if she was not in front she would have a sensation that someone was behind her about to touch her shoulder. Also, she did not want to miss a word, even if she would shake with fright.

Soon the circle in front of the fire was full. Zio Filippo and his wife Cristina sat in the corner, which was considered the best seat because they would not get the draught from the door.

Serafina's mother was busy getting the chestnuts ready to roast on the fire. Her Nonna had some corn in a pot, ready to pop. Once the chestnuts were ready and the corn eaten everyone fell silent. Zio Filippo was telling a story which he said it was the absolute truth.

Serafina made herself comfortable, she moved a little back from the fire, so that her knees were warm but not scorching. She loved the stories that Zio Filippo told. His voice was just right, he knew when to stop for effect, when to go slow in the telling and when to go fast.

'This happened when I was a boy', Zio Filippo began.

'It was a time of great misery just after the first world war. The men had all gone to war and the women managed as best as they could, working hard to make a living so that they could feed their children.

'Some people had to sell their bits of land so that they could eat. When the men came back from the war – the ones that came back, that is – it was a little better but it was still a time of great misery and poverty.

'This is a story of two brothers, Pietro and Pasquale Pia, who lived in Valleporcina. They had been called up as soldiers and went to war. When the war ended they were in the north, I think it was Milan, they were told that the war was over and to 'go home'. There were no trains to take them home, no lorries, no food, just road. The men walked, scavenging as they went along.

'One day the two brothers set out on their own, leaving their fellow soldiers behind. They were walking along a country road, eyes always on the lookout for something to eat, hoping that a lorry or a bus or cart would come by so that they could get a lift for a few miles. Also hoping that a country housewife would take pity on them and give them a meal. They found that if it was just the two of them, this was more likely to happen.

'Then, by great good fortune, they got a lift on a lorry that was going to Frosinone. By then they could almost smell home. Once they arrived they started taking familiar shortcuts or walking across the countryside now that they knew the way.

'Pietro and Pasquale were walking along a country track when they came upon a donkey trotting along in front of them. It had no halter. Pasquale grabbed it by the neck and jumped on its back. Pietro, laughing, was running alongside, saying he wanted to ride on the donkey too. Pietro looked in his backpack and pulled out a rope. He made a halter for the donkey, put the halter on the animal and they both got on his back. The donkey was young and strong and did not seem to mind as it trotted along.'

Zio Filippo stopped talking to eat a few chestnuts. The girl waited for him to go on with his story. When he had his fill Filippo drank a glass of wine to wash them down and then continued.

'The boys had no intention of stealing the donkey, said Zio Filippo, but before they knew it they were in Sora, they thought by now that the donkey could not find his way home, so they went on, taking turns to ride it. And within a few days they were home.

'The young men both had girls waiting for them and before long both were both married and soon children came, one after the other as they did in those days, even though there was a great misery.

'The donkey grew to be a strong, healthy animal, which the brothers shared to do the work about the homestead.

'And this is where the story gets really interesting, said the old man. It was the month of August, a busy time for the wheat harvest.

'Pasquale said to his brother that the day after, he needed the donkey to go to the mill.

'Pietro asked him if he had run out of flour.

'Pasquale said no, he had not run out but was low in flour.

'Pietro said to him, if he still had flour could he go to the mill another day because he needed the donkey to bring the stooks of wheat under cover, in case the weather changed and if it did it would ruin his wheat.

'"No!" barked Pasquale. "I need to go tomorrow – you can have him the day after."

'As he set off, Pietro cursed him. "If it rains tomorrow and spoils my harvest and my children have to go hungry, may you go straight to hell," he shouted after Pasquale, in a rage.

'Pasquale passed through Picinisco with only a few people about; it was dark, the sky building up to a storm. He was coming up to the cemetery which lay just down on the approach to the town. A crack of lightning lit the sky. He stopped. His mind was playing tricks on him, he thought he had seen a dark figure at the gate. Again, a crack of lightning and thunder which lit the sky. He could see a figure of a man standing at the gate of the cemetery. He was looking at him.

'Pasquale held on tight to the reins of the donkey; the beast seemed to be spooked. He looked again to see where the man was but there was no one there. "Strange," he thought.

'He started going down the winding, zig-zag road that led to the bottom of the valley and the mill. As he walked down he thought he could hear someone following him. When he stopped, the footsteps would also stop. He called: "Who's there? Come, we will go together." No answer.

'When he arrived at the mill it was almost light and he looked back to see whether whoever had been behind him would appear. Another bolt of lightning lit the sky, he thought he could see the man sitting in the distance on a rock. He seemed to be waiting. He peered again through the rain but alas the man was gone. This really *was* strange.

'The wheat had been milled and Pasquale started on his way home; the donkey fully laden. It was still raining heavily. The thunder and lightning had lessened, but it was still hard to see the road ahead. On his way back he could hear someone in front of him. He stopped and called. He went on. He was now by the cemetery, walking close to its walls to avoid the pouring rain.

'There was a huge bolt of lightning, followed by an explosion of thunder. He looked up and saw a dark shadow on the roof of the church, and then another crack of thunder! The church steeple was hit by lightning and rocks rained down on poor Pasquale. His last vision was of a dark shadow entering the gate of the cemetery. As it entered, a face turned to looked back at him. It was his own face he saw.

'The donkey trotted on happily with its load still on his back, and made his way home.

'Pietro, with the help of his neighbours, had managed to get his harvest of wheat undercover. He was thanking God for that.

'He had just finished his meal of polenta. He walked outside his house and lit his pipe; from there he could see the road that came down from Fontitune. He saw the donkey with a load, trotting down, but he could not see his brother Pasquale. His heart lurched with fright – he watched the donkey, but still no Pasquale.

'His brother would never return'.

That night the girl was glad that she had her nonna to hold her in a tight embrace. She could imagine a hand coming under the covers to pull her away, a hand to grab her leg from under the bed when she put her foot down, the agony of wanting to go to the toilet but too scared to go because it was outside, too scared to put her foot down on the flag stone floor.

It was the night before the *festa di tutti i morti*, it was bedtime. The girl followed her mother and nonna, too scared to be left alone. They each had small, squat candles, they went to the window, lit the candles. 'This is for you,' they said as they recalled their loved ones.

'Why are you doing this?' the girl asked.

'We put the candles on the window sill so that our dead see the light and can find their way home,' her mother said.

'You mean to say that they will come back from the dead?' Serafina gasped. The girl saw her mother and nonna exchange a look and smile.

The day after it was the feast day. They were all going to Picinisco for the Mass of All Souls' Day, to pray for their departed so that they could rest in peace for another year. After the Mass they would walk down to the cemetery to visit *i morti*, bringing huge bundles of dahlias and chrysanthemums because they had to make sure to visit everyone and leave no one out. The girl followed her mother with a bag of *lumini*. The red candles offered up at graveyards all over Italy.

After all was done they walked up to the *piazza* in Picinisco. Mother had to buy some provisions at the shop. Afterwards, as a treat, she bought the children a drink of *spuma rosa*, a sweet and tasty pop. Serafina looked out from the *piazza*. Down below she could see the cemetery. All lit up, full of flowers and candles. It started to rain, they opened their umbrellas and walked home.

CHAPTER 29

Going to the Mill

THE GIRL WAS sitting at the table. They had just finished eating *sagna e fagioli*, a thing that the girl hated, eggless pasta and beans. She was forced to eat it or go to bed hungry. She would rather have bread and cheese but her mother made her finish her plate.

The girl's mother was saying to her nonna that tomorrow she would go to the mill. She knew there was still plenty of flour, but she would go to make sure. Then there would be enough for the winter; she'd go now before the weather got worse. She also had to buy all the salt and spices for the pig.

'Do you want to come with me for company, Serafina?' asked her mother. Serafina was in a mood and wanted to say no, but she also wanted to go so she nodded her head in agreement. 'In the morning, early!' said her mother. Why did it always have to be early, the girl thought. Could it not be when it was light, at least?

When morning came, she jumped from her bed, running as quickly as possible, to make sure no one grabbed her leg. Quickly, she put on her clothes, splashing her face with cold water.

The girl's mother was down at the stable putting a harness on Peppa. The sack of washed wheat was ready to be loaded on Peppa's back. Zio Filippo was there, helping her mother put the heavy sack on the horse.

When it was on and securely tied, they were ready to go. Zio Filippo gave her mother a list of things he needed from the shop. They walked down the road, the only sound was the clip-clopping of the horse's hooves.

The moon was still up. The people still asleep. Peppa walked behind on a lead. Serafina held onto her mother's hand in case she might see a large white dog.

When they got to Picinisco it was still dark. Her mother did not go through the *piazza* but took what the girl thought was a short-cut, in a back alley that Peppa with her load could just pass through.

When they got to the cemetery the girl hoped that *tutti i morti* were back resting in their place. They took a path off the road, which led down to a deep valley, the path zig-zagged all the way down.

By daylight they reached their destination: a water mill. Because they were early, they were one of the first to be served. The mother brought out some bread and cheese to eat for breakfast. She talked to other people there, some of whom she knew. The girl went for a look round, she was fascinated by all that water. The mill pond and another pond where there were ducks; a bridge over the river with a weeping willow. All things that they did not have in their mountain village.

Before they left to make the return journey, the girl fed Peppa some oats from a bag and afterwards took her to the pond for a drink. The owner of the mill helped her mother to load up the milled flour onto Peppa's back and they were off.

This time, as they passed through the *piazza*, they stopped at the shop. Mother went in to get everything she needed. The girl waited outside. She wanted to ask her mother for some *spuma rosa* but was too shy. On the way up-by her mother gave her a hard sweet to suck – not as good as *spuma rosa* but it would do.

CHAPTER 30

Her Heart Fluttered

AS THEY HAPPILY walked up the road home, the girl talked all the time about this and that, asking questions, on and on. Eventually her mother said: 'Would you give me some peace, I cannot hear myself think and I have a lot to think about.'

'What are you thinking about, Mum? I'm the same. I'm always thinking. Are you thinking about going away, Mum?' And on and on she went.

'Have I not just asked you to give me some peace to think? And actually I was not thinking about going away. I was remembering another time, long ago, that I went to the mill on a day just like today.' Maria sighed as she said this.

'Were you on your own, Mum?' the girl asked.

'No, I was not on my own. I was with your dad.'

'Oh Mum, don't think about it. Tell me about it, just pretend that you are thinking out loud. That way you do all the talking and I will listen, you know I'm a good listener, not just a pesty talker.'

Her mother laughed. 'Yes,' she said, 'you are just a pest.' The girl waited for her mother to speak.

'Well then, you talk!' she exclaimed.

Her mother began. 'It was a day just like today. I got up early. At that time Nonna and I lived with

Zio Domenico, so he got up to help me load the wheat on the donkey and just as I was about to set off, he gave me some money just to spend on myself. I set off feeling happy; one whole day away from the house, all by myself, no babies, no washing, no "Maria, do this," no "Maria, do that," and I had a few pennies. I would buy myself a new scarf, maybe a nice blue one because blue is my favourite colour, as you know.

'Anyway, I was on the road to Picinisco, there are a lot of bends on the road, but as I walked I could hear that there was someone behind me, also with a donkey. I would stop a while, hoping they would catch up. Then I would walk on; because of the bends I could not see who it was. Eventually, on the long bit of straight road in the distance, I could see that it was Raffaele and I waited for him.'

Maria knew the boy well. Of course she did, did she not know everyone in the village well? Too well; every word said was repeated, every quarrel talked about. Every prank laughed over, every act criticised, every smile admired, every pain and bereavement, shared. Theirs was a small community of shepherds, set apart from the people in the plains who tilled land that was not their own. They gave half of their harvest to Don Michele or Don Pierino, who between them owned nearly all the land in the plains.

Maria had played with Raffaele when they were children, roaming the mountain to gather firewood. In the autumn they'd searched for chestnuts under layers of leaf and mould. They had looked after grazing goats on the mountainside together. But Raffaele was three years older than Maria, soon he joined other young men, to play different games. He had been called up to join the army and had been to war, spending eighteen months in a prisoner of war camp. When he came back he was weak and thin; it took him a while to get back to good health. He had no mother or father to pamper him and feed him well. That had been two years ago.

Maria had not seen him for a while but she knew that he was in much the same position as herself. The youngest of the family and at the beck and call of all of his brothers and sisters.

'I had not seen your dad for a while,' the girl's mother went on. 'And as he approached me for the first time I thought to myself how nice-looking he was. He had put on some weight and it really suited him. He came up to me and smiled. He pushed his hat to the back of his head and with just that action, I fell in love with him. He did not know that his smile was one of the things that made him attractive. It was in one way tender and in another, vulnerable, it softened the piercing look of his eyes, with that smile I felt the first little tug at my heartstrings.

'Every time I pass this point in the road, where we are now, just here,' and she moved a few paces up, 'this is where I felt that little flip of my heart.' She laughed as she said this and said: 'I blushed at that moment – a flame of red swept up my face. I looked down and walked ahead hoping he had not seen it. I was embarrassed. It was only Raffaele, I was being so stupid but he had seen me getting all flustered and let me walk ahead until I'd recovered. When he caught up with me to walk at my side, he looked at me with his blue eyes, really looked at me as if he had just met me for the first time. He later told me that it had been the same for him. When he looked at me it was then he had seen not just little Maria but a young woman, a beautiful young woman, he said,' and she laughed again.

'Did he kiss you then?' the girl asked, all excited.

'Of course not,' her mother said. 'Kisses are for when you are married.' But she went silent with a smile still on her face.

'Well, go on, Mum, what happened then?' Her mother did not hear. 'Mum, go on then,' the girl nudged her.

'I then asked him why he was looking so tired, his clothes all crumpled, why he had been so late to set off to go to the mill. Talk between us had always been easy; he would talk of things that would make us laugh; easy banter. But somehow he went really quiet, deep in his own thoughts. After a while he started to tell me he had only slept a couple of hours. He had been to see his girlfriend Teresa at Valleporcina, then a dance had started up. He had stayed longer than he had wanted to, he knew he was going to the mill in the morning. Teresa would just not let him go. She wanted him to speak to her father to ask him if he could marry her. But *a fare l'amore* was really nice and Teresa was a great girl.

'She kept pushing him to speak to her dad and he would say to her that he would do it next time he saw him, and then he would put it off. Telling me this, a pained and thoughtful look would pass his face.

'Getting married was a serious business,' he said.

'I knew what the look said. It said: "I have no house, I have no animals, I have no land. I have no mother or father to help me. How can I ask her to marry me? Her father would say no.'"

'Were you upset that he had a girlfriend?' the girl asked her mother.

'Well,' said her mother, 'a little bit. But I tried to not let him see that.'

'Did he kiss you then?' the girl asked.

'What is this all about kissing, no kissing until you get married and you remember that, young lady,' her mother said.

The girl knew that this was not true because she had seen the girls and boys *a fare l'amore*, kissing. The girl and her friends would sometimes follow couples who were *a fare l'amore* to see what they were up to and she had seen them kissing but she did not say this to her mother. By this time, they had arrived home. Serafina thought to herself that she would ask her mum to tell her more another time.

CHAPTER 31

Killing Mr Pig

THE GIRL WAS sitting by the fire. She was so cold. There was a good flame to the fire, but no matter how close she sat, her back was always cold. She had on her thick new woollen vest that her nonna had knitted. It itched against her skin, she wanted to scratch her back. She wriggled and said, 'Could you scratch my back, Nonna?'

Her grandmother pushed her out of the way. She had a black sooty pot which was filled with food for the pig: small potatoes from the allotment, oats, apples, crushed corn, all to be cooked for his highness Mr Pig. He would be given as much as he could eat so he would get as fat as possible. He ate well, that pig, a hot meal every day. Sometimes the family would have bread and cheese for their meal but the pig always got a hot meal.

'This will be his last meal,' said the girl's nonna. 'The day after tomorrow is the feast of Mr Pig.' The girl knew exactly what she meant. She had seen other pigs being killed. In the village they would take turns to do this. They would help each other. The girl was not much bothered; she was a country girl and she did love *prosciutto* and sausages.

Her mother and grandmother were really busy in preparation, all the ingredients they needed to make sausages: ham, bacon, lard, everything was used, nothing wasted. It had to last a whole year. She had heard her nonna say many times that the sign of a good housewife was whether she could make the pig last a year and have a little left over for the new year.

The day arrived, misty and cold, ideal weather. On the little courtyard beside the steps that came up to the house, a low platform of wooden planks was made ready. A log fire was burning with a large cauldron of water on a steady boil. The steam floated in the cold air.

The girl's big cousin Narduccio and Zio Filippo were already there. Soon Maria's brother Luigi arrived to help his sister. He had come up from the plains. He knew that Maria did not have her husband to help, so he had made the journey especially. They needed another man, so Serafina was sent to call Zio Pasquale, Maria's uncle.

All was ready, they were just waiting for the man that would actually kill the pig. He was a travelling man who would go around the villages. He knew where to put the knife to get a quick and clean death. When he arrived the girl looked on fascinated, he had bright red hands. She wanted to see everything. She was like that, the girl: curious. 'Nosy!' her mother said, '*Sempre mezze i piedi*' – always in the way. Some other people also came to help or just to watch.

How To Kill Mr Pig:

The job of the men.

Step one: Mother went into the stable with a basket of corn – the pig had not been fed the previous day ready for slaughter. So Mr Pig followed the basket of corn quite happily.

Step two: The four men, Narduccio, Zio Filippo, Zio Luigi and Zio Pasquale all grabbed a leg each and toppled the pig on to the wooden platform, while other people helped to hold the squealing animal down.

Step three: The man with the red hands quickly put the point of his sharp knife in the pig's throat. Blood came flooding out. The girl's nonna was ready with a basin with thick slices of bread at the bottom to catch the blood.

Poor pig, thought the girl as he gave up his last struggle, stopped twitching, and everyone let go. The girl watched, sad that it had to be this way. Now the pig was dead, the men set about cleaning the pig. The cauldron of water was boiling; it was someone's job to keep the fire roaring. The men would take jugs full of boiling water and steep the feet of the animal, then with a hook pull out its hooves. The children would pick them up and put them on their fingers walking around on all fours, making grunting noises. In the cauldron of boiling water there were sacks, and with tongs they picked up these steaming sheets and covered the body of the pig, adding further jugs of boiling water to the wrapped carcass as required.

After a while they would take away the sacks and scrape the dark skin off to reveal nice pink skin underneath. With a sharp blade, one of the long ones which they sharpened on a leather strap, they would give the pig a full and complete shave to remove all the black hair. Then a good wash all over and all was done for now.

Next they had to take the pig up the steps to the kitchen. This was not easy as the pig was well-fed, fat and heavy. So it required all hands, men and women, to take it up the steps into the kitchen and hang it on a hook in the ceiling that was there just for this occasion (all the houses in the village had one).

Now it was the turn again of the man with the red hands. The pig was hanging upside down with a big basin under it. The man slit the pig right down the middle, from head to foot, and out plopped all his insides.

Everyone exclaimed how nice it looked, lots of fat and nice pink flesh. The job of the man with the red hands was done. He was paid and went away after a glass of wine.

The girl's mother had prepared a big pot of *baccalà* (salted cod) and potatoes cooked in tomato sauce, and lots of olive oil for lunch. She had also put in a handful of dried prunes for sweetness and to make it go further, and there was lots of bread to dip in the sauce. Everyone that had helped sat around the table and ate.

Now was the job of the women.

Maria and Nanduccio's young wife Filomena (they had married that summer) between them picked up the basin holding all the innards of the animal and went to the fountain where there was plenty of running water. They went to wash everything; the guts would be used for casing sausages, the bladder would hold melted fat, which would harden. Everything was used for something.

The pig was left hanging for a couple of days before it was cut up. In the meantime, the blood pudding was made. The basin with the bread and blood had all been mashed up. The bread stopped the blood from coagulating. Lots of other things were added: sugar, chilli, orange peel (the children would eat the flesh of the oranges, as only the peel was required). Years later,

Serafina would hear her father say that black pudding needed thirteen special ingredients. Anyway, when they were ready and in their casing they were plonked into a cauldron of boiling water to cook. When they were done, they were hung up to dry.

Absolutely nothing was wasted; if by chance one or two of the blood puddings would burst and ooze into the water, even this would not be thrown away. Mother would get handfuls of wheat, crack and grind it on her grinding stone, throw this in the pot, put the pot back on the fire and cook the meal until it was thick like a porridge. When it was cold she would cut it into slices and fry it. They would eat this hot or cold.

Everything had its own process: the leg for *prosciutto*, belly for bacon and lard of course for cooking. An abundance of sausages would be made. These were summer foods. The ears, the cheeks, the trotters, the tongue, the tail, the skin were all salted; these were all winter foods. They would be eaten with cabbage, potatoes and beans.

The house smelt of good things: pepper, sugar, lemons, oranges, chilli, cinnamon, nutmeg, paprika, fennel seeds, bay leaves. Does that make thirteen?

Different sausages needed different spices. When all was done all the fat and trimmings would be rendered down to produce thick creamy fat which would be used to preserve the sausages. The sausages when dry were put in a steel bin. The fat would be poured into the bin until it was full. The fat would go hard and the sausages would be good for years, kept in a cool place.

Lastly all the crispy bits that were left would be tossed with a little salt, and fried, delicious to eat with bread that evening.

And that was the life and death of Mr Pig. Funny how the girl would remember every detail all her life, but most of all she remembered the smell of spices, fruit and blood.

CHAPTER 32

Sitting by the Fire Daydreaming

THE GIRL WOULD sit by the fire and look into its flames. She tried to see into the future. What would life be like in a faraway country? Why did they have to go? She liked it where she was, she liked going to school in the summer and winter.

She recalled last year, which was her first year at winter school. All the children looked on her as a stranger, the daughter of a shepherd, but she soon got to know them, they spoke the same language. They had their different ways of life, but these too were country people. They worked the land but they stayed in one place, not like the girl's family.

She remembered last year it was Easter-time and the children at school brought eggs for the teacher tied in a cloth, five to ten eggs. The girl told her mother this and she wanted to bring eggs too. She did not want to be different from the rest.

The girl was mortified when her mother gave her two eggs tied in a hanky to bring to the teacher because she did not have any more. Maybe going to *la Scozia* would be the same as going down-by: new people, different way of doing things, to be looked at as a stranger. These were all things that the girl and her family were already used to.

Her mother and father would do their best to show the country people that they were honest folk. They would always ask if they could graze their sheep on fields that were lying fallow and would always pay for pasture they rented. If someone was kind and helped, they would give them fresh cheese and *ricotta*.

At Easter-time her father would give the owner of the homestead they were staying at a young lamb. Her father always said to his children not to touch anything that was not theirs. He always said: 'When you live among strangers it's up to you to prove that you are an honest and hardworking person. You want always to be able to hold your head high. If you do that, you can go again next year and the next, people will respect you.'

CHAPTER 33

A Time of Waiting

AFTER THE PIG had been killed, and with everything else in its place, those still in the village took what they would eat in the winter and left to join the rest of their families. When Rita left with her brother, the two girls clung to each other, crying bitterly, thinking this was no ordinary goodbye. Next summer they would not be together to do what nine-year-old girls do; perhaps no longer playmates but young women, looking at the world in a different way, but always together.

The girl's mother was waiting to hear from her husband. When could they join him? She would go to Picinisco to check if there was a letter. Afterwards, she would go to the dressmaker where she was getting a few things made for herself and Serafina. She would go to the market to get things for the boys, trying to stretch her money as far as possible. They needed so much, shoes and a coat each. It was cold in *la Scozia*. She would go to the post office to see if there was a letter with instructions for her. Disappointment when there was nothing; elation when word came from Raffaele.

And one day there it was, a letter saying that a friend of Chiarina was coming to Picinisco (Maria knew her). She would bring the tickets for the journey to Scotland. They were to leave on the 18th of December. So soon! She was not expecting it to be so soon. The letter went on with instructions; what to bring; what to leave behind. One of the things Raffaele said she had to do she did not like at all – it would cost money she did not have.

The girl was watching her mother as she read. What was wrong? Her mother looked happy then sad; she walked up and down. They sat down on the bench in the *piazza*.

'What's wrong, Mum?' said the girl.

'There is nothing wrong, we are going to your dad, soon, before Christmas.'

They were walking home. Her mother deep in thought, the girl also thoughtful. They walked in silence for a while, the girl looking at the snow-covered mountains. She was remembering all her playmates, all the games, all the events of the summer. She felt sad that she would leave all this behind, leave her beloved nonna.

She looked at her mother. 'Mum, why have you and dad decided to leave all this,' she waved her hand to include her world. 'We are happy here, we have plenty to eat, we have our house, our friends and family. Why?'

Her mother stopped and looked at her daughter. She was thinking the same thing: why were they doing this? She thought of all the reasons she had talked about with her husband, and they seemed good reasons at the time.

'Serafina,' she said, 'the life of a shepherd is not a good one. It is hard work, dirty work, we have to move about like gypsies. The world is changing. We want more for you and your brothers. We have this opportunity to go where Zia Chiarina is. She will help us. We will not be completely alone and your father has said that if we don't like it, we can come back. So don't worry, everything will be alright.'

But in spite of her words Maria was worried. Raffaele wanted this more than she wanted it. She knew her husband was ambitious to get on. He could not forget the hard times of the past. He was afraid and did not ever want to go back there. He never wanted his children ever to have to go through what he had gone through so he took every opportunity in life. That was the reason why they were now one of the better-off families in the village – because he took every opportunity. They had started their married life with nothing.

The girl looked at her mother. She knew that she was deep in thought. Serafina said, 'Mum, do you remember when we went to the mill and you were thinking and I asked you to think out loud, and you told me about you and Dad going to the mill? Could you do that again? Think out loud, that is? You know I am a good listener.' Her mother laughed and patted her head.

'You are funny,' she said, putting her hand around Serafina's shoulders to give her a squeeze.

'Well, what were you thinking about this time?' asked the girl.

'You know, you have asked me why we are going away?' answered her mother. 'Well, your dad wants what is best for you because he had a hard time himself as a boy. They were very poor, they were a big family. He was the youngest, his mother was always ill. She died when he was twelve years old and a few years later his father died too. Then his older brothers and sisters all got married. They took all that there was and there was nothing left for him.

'When we got married,' her mother went on, 'we had nothing, we lived with his sister, Zia Serafina, and her husband Giovanni. Then the winter came and everyone went their own way down-by. Serafina shared what there was in the house between them, a bit of lard, some oil, some cheese, half a sack of flour and eight sheep, which was his share of the herd, and that was it.

'My family was not talking to me because I had shamed them by marrying your dad without their permission. Nonna, though, would bring some things to me and leave them at the door.

'One day I met up with Nonna and she said to me that she could not help me. She said that she had put a little bit of money aside for me but when she went to get it from where she had left it, it was no longer there, someone had taken it. She cried when she said this. And that was it.'

Maria was remembering; almost everyone had left the village for the winter, there were only a few old people that were not going down-by.

What would they do all winter? What would they eat? They had plenty of wood, so at least they would not freeze. In the winter it was impossible to find work of any kind on the mountain. They would lie in bed all day and sleep as much as they could.

One morning she woke up and Raffaele was not there beside her.

When she got up he was not there, he had gone away somewhere. He did not come back until it was dark. She had sat by the fire waiting, waiting, waiting for him. Her heart ached. How she loved him, she would be happy to die with him as long as she was in his arms.

When he came back they sat and ate their *polenta* with a spoonful of oil. Their hunger appeased, she asked him where he had been. He said to her, 'We can't stay here and starve.' He said he had been to Picinisco to see if there was any work, any kind of work.

While he was there he had met Giuseppe Faccenda from the village of La Rocca. He had fifty sheep. This year he could not go down-by because his father was dying and he could not move him and he could not leave him alone.

'Anyway,' Raffaele went on, 'I said to him that I would take his sheep down-by and any money we made we would share. And!' he said with a rare smile on his face, 'he has agreed.'

The very next day Raffaele had gone down-by to look for a steading where they could stay for free. Sometimes country people would be happy to have shepherds for the winter. They would use the manure for their fields.

He came back and they packed what few things they had: one fork, one spoon each, a few clothes, any food there was in the house. Raffaele rolled it all inside a mattress, tied it up with a rope and put it on his back. Maria filled a basket with some potatoes and beans that her mother had left at the door, put the basket on her head and away they went with their eight sheep to meet Giuseppe Faccenda outside Picinisco, where he would hand over his own flock.

The homestead Raffaele had found was at Sant' Elia. A good place, he said, lots of fallow land where the people would let them graze their flock, if they were careful not to let the sheep damage the trees. Cassino was not too far away, where he could go to sell cheese and *ricotta*. He could walk there, save money on bus fares. When they arrived where they were to stay, Raffaele said it was the best he could get. It was a hut. Maria stared, trying not to show her disappointment: two rooms side by side, one for the animals and one for them. But the worst was still to come. When they walked in, there was a roar.

'What's that?' she said to him. 'What's that noise?'

'This used to be a mill,' he said. The water passed under the hut before it got to the wheel. The room was cold and damp but at least it had a small fireplace and they soon had a fire going to cook their polenta. They shared the polenta, eating it straight from the pot.

Raffaele had gone out to see what he could find that would do for a bed. They did not want to put their mattress on the damp floor.

Maria cleaned the hut the best she could, but her mind was not on it. All she could think of was how she was going to tell Raffaele that soon there would be another mouth to feed. She did not have the heart to tell him that she was expecting a baby. He would worry for her, for the child. He came back with some planks of wood, which he said he had got from the old mill. He also had some bricks, and with the bricks and wood he made a platform. He put the mattress on top and that was their bed.

'There,' he said, 'off the damp floor. Shall we try it?' He sat on the bed: 'Come and sit beside me.' They made love.

Afterwards he passed his hand over her body. He paused on her belly and passed his hand over again, and sat up to look at her, their eyes locked. He bent down to kiss her.

'It is alright,' he said, 'we will manage.'

'Mum, you are not thinking out loud anymore; I can see that from your face, you are deep in thought but not speaking,' said the girl.

'I was just remembering our first winter together, it was really hard,' her mother continued the tale. 'We had no money at all, so that when we went down-by we could not buy any pasture. We had to beg people to let the sheep graze on their land or we would pay them with a little bit of cheese or *ricotta*. We would eat *polenta* every day. We would not eat any cheese or *ricotta* because we had to sell it.

'By this time I was expecting a baby, your brother Fortunato. Anyway, want to hear a funny story that happened when we were down-by and I was expecting Fortunato?

'I am sure you have heard people say that when you are expecting a baby and you take a fancy for something special to eat, then you have got to have it or your baby could have something wrong with it. You have heard of that, haven't you?'

Serafina nodded her head, yes, she had.

'Well,' said her mother, 'I took this fancy for cherries. I could not get this thought out of my mind. Your dad asked me what was wrong, why was I in a bad mood. This went on for weeks. Eventually, one

day, Raffaele came home and I was by the fire crying.
I told him why.

'Next day he came home with an orange. "I don't
want an orange', I said.

'Next day he unwrapped his handkerchief: there
was a pear. "I don't want it," I said. A couple of days
later he somehow got hold of some grapes. When
he showed me them, I pushed them out of his hand.
They went flying into the fireplace. Your dad looked
on in despair because at that time of the year there
was no way he could get cherries. He looked at the
burning grapes and licked his lips because he had not
even tasted them before giving them to me.

'Next day your dad went out with the sheep and
everyone he met and every house he passed he asked
if they had any cherries or where he could find one for
his wife who was expecting. Eventually he asked at a
house, expecting the usual answer. But this time the lady
of the house said wait a minute, she would have a look.

'She came back with three wrinkled cherries,
preserved in spirits. She wrapped them in a piece of
paper and gave them to your dad.

'Your dad could not wait for the time to come, that
he could herd the sheep back home so he could give
me the cherries.

'I was sitting by the fireplace, watching some beans
cooking. Raffaele sat beside me and took the little
wrapper out of his pocket to reveal the three cherries.
I looked at them: I could not believe my eyes.

I quickly popped one into my mouth and ate it.
I remember this wonderful feeling of peace and
happiness. I flung my arms around your dad and

laughed. "You can eat the other two," I said to him. "I don't want them".'

Maria laughed: the girl laughed with her.

'That is a funny story, Mum,' the girl said.

They continued in silence, each with their own thoughts. Maria was remembering that night she and her husband had clung to each other, both happy even in their misery. Their child would be alright. The winter passed soon; it was time to get ready to go up-by. They did not want to leave it too late: they wanted the baby to be born at home in Fontitune.

They counted their money from the sale of cheese and *ricotta*, and a few lambs. They had arranged to meet Giuseppe Faccenda outside Picinisco so he could take his flock back. They shared the money. Raffaele took his own eight sheep and five lambs, shook hands with Giuseppe and asked if the bargain they had made had suited him. Giuseppe said that he was more than happy. He had never expected to get so much money and a well-fed and healthy herd. And for this he gave Raffaele two more of his lambs.

So, then they had eight sheep, seven lambs and some money. They were delighted.

They were making their way home when they passed the post office and someone called out that there was a letter for Raffaele Crolla. It was from Chiarina. Raffaele gave it to Maria to read.

> Dear Brother,
>
> I hope this letter finds you well and Maria too.
>
> I have heard that you were down-by for the winter.
>
> I also heard that Maria is expecting a baby – *Auguri* (congratulations). Hope all goes well with her.

Dear brother, I know that when you go back to Fontitune you will have nowhere to live because our brother Domenico has moved with all his family into our old family home and there will be no room for you.

I have bought the house that belonged to Giovanni Crolla because, as you know, he is now in Scotland and says that he will never return to Fontitune, and he wanted to sell it. I paid 600 thousand *lira* for the house and some bits of land.

Zio Filippo has the key for the house. You can go and live there and use the land.

Don't worry about paying me back because I can wait for however long it takes for you to get the money. Five years, ten years, it does not matter, so don't worry about it now.

Lots of love and kisses for you and your wife. Love and kisses to all the rest.

Your sister,

Chiarina

They stood in astonishment. Then they flung their arms around each other and cried with joy and happiness. They had a house, they had some land, they had eight sheep and seven lambs that would soon be sheep. They would have a healthy baby. What joy and happiness!

'Are you doing it again, Mum? Thinking but not talking,' the girl asked, pulling on Maria's hand. They both laughed and went on to talk of other things, and before they knew it they were at home.

The girl could see her mother had so much to do. She washed and scrubbed the children, put on their best clothes and took them to Picinisco to have their photographs taken for their passports. She took the photographs to the *Sindaco* (town mayor), so he could order the passports, as she had no idea how to do this. She put some cheese and bacon in a basket to take to him as an offering of thanks.

One night the girl was sitting at the table, they had just eaten. She heard her mother say to her nonna: 'I have run out of money. I don't know what to do. Raffaele wants me to do so much, he doesn't realise how the money goes.'

The girl's nonna listened and then she said, 'Why don't you take some of the pig to the shop in Picinisco and sell it? The *prosciutto* is too fresh, you can't take it with you.'

'No,' answered her daughter. 'The things I can't take with me I'll leave for you.'

'Oh, I can't eat such rich stuff, take it and sell it, you can use the money,' her mother insisted.

All was ready and waiting for the day of departure. A few days before they were to leave, the girl's mother went to Picinisco on her own. She was away most of the day. When she came back they were all sitting by the fire; outside snowflakes descended on the sleepy village.

Their mother walked in shyly. She was not carrying anything, which was unusual because when she went to Picinisco she always came back with something. The girl's nonna stood up.

'Let me see, then,' she said. They all looked up in expectation. Her mother took her headscarf off. She had had her long beautiful hair cut off as Raffaele had requested. At the front it was the same but at the back it was short and curly. Nonna cried, Maria smiled.

CHAPTER 34

Peppa

THE DAY CAME for her dad's cousin Michele, who had bought Peppa, to come and get her. Fortunato tried not to cry and be a man about it, but the girl could see that it was breaking his heart.

He went into the stable to give the mare a good rub down with the special brushes that he had begged his father to buy at the market in Atina. He fed her a bag of oats. Then he said that he would like a last ride on her. Mother was about to say no. Then she thought better of it and let him go for a short ride.

When he came back, Michele was already there. He looked at the horse, admired its sleek rump, took the reins and off he went, up the road to his house. The man was staying in the village for a while. He had come to spend Christmas with his parents who had not gone down-by with the rest of the family. While he was at home in the village, he was cleaning out his stable. He would load manure in a special harness on Peppa and take it to his fields. He would have to pass the girl's house on every journey.

When Peppa came to the house, she thought that she was home. She would stop at the gate, neigh, and toss her head. She did not want to go any further. Her new owner would whip her to keep her going. Peppa would take this personally and lift her hind hoof to kick, which was something she had never done before, but then again, she had never been whipped. Fortunato could not bear to look.

CHAPTER 35
Journey to *la Scozia*

THE NIGHT BEFORE they were to leave, everything was in the trunk, the cases packed, three wicker bags full of food ready for the journey. All goodbyes had been said, so they went to bed early to try to sleep. Maria got up and was surprised that her mother was not up. She was always first up to light the fire. She was awake, their eyes met. Maria lit the fire, put the water on for tea then went to wake the boys. When the boys were ready she went to Serafina. She was sleeping; soundly clasped in her nonna's arms.

The girl's nonna shook her. 'Time to get up,' she said.

'No... I'm staying here with you.' Serafina clung tighter to her nonna.

'Come on now, you have to go with your family, your father is waiting for you.'

'No, no, no,' she cried. 'I'm not going!'

Zio Luigi arrived with Middiuccio, and then Zio Filippo and the man who had bought Peppa. They had come to help with the trunk and cases.

'Come, Serafina, you have to get dressed now.' Her mother pulled her away from the arms of her nonna. By this time the boys were crying too.

Once she was dressed and ready to go, Maria went to her mother and lay down beside her, embraced her, kissed her. She wanted to say so much. She loved her so much. They had been together all of her life but she must be brave. She must go.

'Go now,' said her mother. 'I will pretend that you are going down-by and will see you soon.'

The girl thought that her heart would break as she walked to the bottom of the village where the car was. Then they were all packed in the car and off they went, rattling down the road.

The girl looked back. The snow-covered mountains, the village. They passed the last house, then the chestnut tree with the Madonnina, Picinisco, then past the cemetery. Her mother made the sign of the cross as they went by. Then Atina, where there was the Monday market. Then they came to Cassino, where she had seen the tallest man in the world; and all that was her world.

When they got to Rome's train station there were so many people. The girl held on tight to her mother's skirt. She was terrified of getting lost.

Zio Luigi and Middiuccio helped Maria with the luggage. The trunk was posted, so she would see it again in 'Dover'. They helped her to her platform, making sure she had all her papers for the third time. When the train arrived, they helped her to her coach.

'Please take care of Mamma, don't leave her on her own, tell her how much I love her. So many things I wanted to say to her but could not,' Maria told her brother, and so much more, while they waited for the train to go.

The time came for those who were not travelling to get off the train. Maria and Luigi embraced.

'Be careful,' he said, 'ask for help if you need it. Don't worry about Mamma, I will take care of her. Write when you arrive.'

Another embrace: a love that would last a lifetime. Maria and the children waved from the window until they could not see the familiar faces anymore.

In the coach, there were also two men, both in dark clothes with shirts and ties. They spoke to each other in a strange language. Serafina sat by the window, everything went by so quickly that she was feeling quite sick; she turned her back to the window trying not to look. Vincenzo soon made friends with the two men. They were laughing at him, finding him amusing. The men were about her father's age. They looked like her English cousins, only they were both really thin. They crossed their legs and smoked.

Maria brought out some food, the things that would perish first: boiled eggs and chicken, bread and a jar of her pickle. She offered some to the *signori* but they said no, they were going to eat in the restaurant and left to go there.

As the girl was eating, she looked out of the window again. All she could see was a huge expanse of grey water and far away a grey sky. Where had everything gone? Just water and sky!

'That's the sea,' said her mother. She had never seen the sea before. The girl was scared, she looked to her mother for reassurance but Maria looked scared too.

When it got dark the men went away to sleep somewhere else, so they spread out the best they could and slept on the seats. All of the next day they were still on the train. Her mother spoke with the *signori*. They were going to *Londra*. They asked Maria where she was going and told her not to worry, they would help.

'When we get off this train in Paris, we will board another that will take us to Calais.' Maria had been told that was what she had to do, but now she was having to do it – alone with three children and luggage, strange places and an unknown language. She had been told to always hold out her ticket, showing her destination, to a porter.

'I'm a woman, I have never been away from home. How could my husband put me through this?' she cried. She wiped her eyes as tears came. The girl, seeing her mother cry, huddled beside her. Fortunato looked on with big eyes; only Vincenzo played on.

The men reassured her.

'We will help you as far as *Londra* and after that, one more train and you will arrive at *Tinburgo*.'

The girl thought that the journey would never end. They were waiting to get on the ship, so they could cross the sea. The girl thought of home, thought of her nonna, they were going so far away, she would never see her again. When they were settled on the ship, it finally set off. It moved up and down under her feet. She looked over the rail; all grey, where had the colours gone?

She looked at the other passengers who were all chatting, laughing, women smoking: a thing she had never seen before. They would sit and cross their legs like the men, with their legs showing.

Now they were on land, waiting with a big crowd of people. They all had to go through a gate.

They were standing in a big space and a man was speaking to her mother. Her mother looked to one of the *signori*. He said, 'They are asking what is in the trunk and the cases.'

The *signore* then said: 'They want you to open your trunk.' Mother opened the trunk. The man looked in quickly, made a face and closed the lid. Half of Mr Pig was in there, and lots of *pecorino* cheese. The man moved them on.

The next stop was *Londra*. This was where they were to say another goodbye, to the kind *signori*. They were going to a place called 'Battersea,' in London. They put the little family in a taxi with all their things, bound for King's Cross station where they would take the train to Edinburgh. Mother said thank you a hundred times to the *signori*. She asked the children to kiss them and say thank you, too. She shook their hands and said, *'Per l'anima dei tuoi morti.'*

At King's Cross, Maria showed her ticket to a porter and, sure enough, he took them to the platform for Edinburgh.

They were on a night train. Outside, the rain sliding down the window panes; inside, all steamed up. Maria did her best to clean the children with a wet cloth. They ate what was left of the food. They were all so tired. Vincenzo would not settle; he cried and cried until he fell asleep. Maria closed her eyes but it was a long time before she too slept.

Finally the train arrived at Edinburgh and Waverley Station. The girl stood on the platform with her family. She looked around for her father, and saw a man with a big grey flapping coat running towards them. Vincenzo took off towards him, his little legs going as fast as they could.

Maria and Fortunato also ran to meet him. The girl stood and looked about: was this it then? All the buildings black and grey.

They left the station in a taxi. Their father was taking them to their new home. Then the girl saw a tall pointed tree with twinkling lights in all the colours.

She smiled; maybe it was not too bad. At least the trees in Edinburgh were colourful.

CHAPTER 36

They Were Lucky

THEY WERE LUCKY to arrive in a land where the people were kind and lent a hand.

It was now five years since they had left their mountain home. It had been an eventful five years. Raffaele had worked for his sister Chiarina but was now getting itchy feet. He wanted to do something for himself – he had not come to *la Scozia* to work for someone else. His independent spirit, the self-reliance he had learned on the mountain, pushed him to get on.

Maria had worked too, in fact she had two jobs. A day job at Duncan's chocolate factory, and at weekends she worked in a local restaurant washing dishes.

The children too were self-reliant; they looked after themselves while their parents worked. They would roam the streets playing with other children and soon learned to speak English. In the flat below them lived another family, Mr and Mrs Mackenzie. They took the young Italian family under their wing and were very kind. They had two daughters, Margaret and Elizabeth, who would knock on the girl's door and ask if she wanted to come out to play.

In the summer, when it was light late in the day, they would stay out till it was dark. The girl and her brothers had no sense of time. Their father would say they had to be at home by nine o'clock. They would go home when it was dark. On one occasion, someone had told their father that they had seen his children playing in the streets very late. Raffaele left his work to get home by nine o'clock to see what they were up to. When they arrived home their father was already there. 'I thought I told you to be home by nine o'clock,' he said as he took his belt out of his trousers. There was no protecting hand from her nonna this time and both Serafina and Fortunato got a licking. Vincenzo looked on thinking he would be next but Raffaele decided it was not his fault, his brother and sister had been told to look after him.

The back streets of Leith Walk were full of children of all ages playing. It was just like Fontitune so the children felt at home. Serafina, though, missed the mountains – the colour of the sky, the light, the summer heat. Most of all she missed her nonna. It took a long time to get used to sleeping on her own. At night she would curl up and cry. She started to suck her thumb for comfort.

Then one day, about a year after they had left their village, the girl came home from school. Her father was already there for his three-hour break before he had to go back to work. He was preparing the evening meal that they would eat when Maria came back from the factory at half-past five. There was a letter from Italy, it was from Zio Luigi. Raffaele handed it to his daughter to read. Serafina sat at the round table in the middle of the small kitchen. She opened the letter, it started in the usual way.

'Dear Sister and Brother-in-Law, I hope this letter finds you all well and that life in *Tinburgo* is good for you. But, my dearest sister, I am sorry to say that I have some bad news for you. Our beloved Mother has passed away. She passed peacefully in her sleep in *L'ara Cullucia*.'

The girl dropped the letter. She shouted, 'No! No! No! Not my nonna! Not my nonna!' The boys and Raffaele were crying. The girl's father put his arm round her to console her. 'I knew I would not see her again,' she cried.

Serafina's father put the food at the back of the cooker and turned off the gas. He sat at the table with his children around him, and drying his tears he looked at the clock. It was four o'clock. Maria would be back in a while. He spoke to the children. 'Your mamma will be back soon. How are we going to tell her?'

'I could cook the meal now and have it ready.'

'We will tell her after she has eaten, you know how hungry she is when she gets home.'

'Yes, we will do that, but we all have to play our part. I will cook the food; you will stop crying and go and wash your faces and comb your hair. Then come to set the table so that we will eat as soon as she gets here, and after we have eaten, we will tell her. *Va bene?*'

The children nodded and went to do as they were told.

Soon all was ready. They sat around the table and watched the clock. Mamma should be back any minute now. 'Try to look normal,' said their father as they heard footsteps on the stairs. The key was in the door and Raffaele ladled the food on to the plates. 'Come straight in, the food is on the table,' he called.

Maria walked in, glad to be home after a long day. She walked into the kitchen, took out the bar of hazelnut chocolate which she had in her pocket and put it on the table. She took her coat off and put it on the back of the chair, and sat down to eat. The girl and her brothers sat to eat also. Maria was usually really hungry when she came back from work so she put her head down to eat. Soon she was finished and sat back. She looked at the children, she looked at their plates with food still on them. She looked at the chocolate – no fighting over it? She looked at her husband who was looking straight at her, his eyes sad and dark.

A lump came to her throat; something was wrong. Relief as Raffaele was here, as were the children, so she relaxed a little. 'What's wrong? What has happened?' she asked her husband.

'We got a letter from Luigi today, I'm afraid there is bad news. Mamma is gone. She has passed away. I'm so sorry,' he said.

Maria was stunned, she looked at her children who were sobbing. She stood up, her husband stood also. She went into her bedroom and threw herself on her bed, tossing this way and that. 'Oh Mamma!' she said. 'I will never see you again. I'm so sorry that I left you when you needed me most. You were always there for me but I was not there for you.' On and on she went. She would not be touched by her husband, blaming him for taking her away from her mother.

The girl sat by her mother and sobbed for her nonna. They cried together because they had loved her most. Next morning the girl's mother was dressed all in black to mourn the passing of her mother.

It was about this time, shortly after her grandmother died, that Serafina discovered books. She liked school and learned quickly, she had a teacher that she loved – Miss Kelly, a young woman about twenty-five years old. Every day she would give the girl something to take home and read. Every morning the girl would bring it back and Miss Kelly would have something else for her. One morning the teacher was chatting with a colleague and Serafina approached with her book. The teacher turned to the other and laughed.

'Have you met the wee Italian girl? She reads a book a day and I have nothing left to give her.'

Her colleague smiled and said, 'Why don't you join the library, lass?' The girl did, and it opened up a whole new world for her.

CHAPTER 37
Erica

THE NONNA WALKED out from the kitchen, wiping her hands on a piece of kitchen paper. It was a hot, still midsummer's day, the heat shimmering and hazy. She sat and enjoyed the view. She would never get used to its beauty. She had been shooed out of the kitchen. She tried to help fill the dishwasher but was told firmly to sit down because that was the agreement, she had made the lunch and everyone else would clean up.

No sooner had she sat down than her granddaughter Erica sat down beside her. She pulled the little girl's soft warm body close to her and gave her a big smacking kiss on her brown cheeks. The child pulled away, it was too hot for cuddles and she knew how much her nonna liked hugs. Holding her nonna's hand, the child said in her sweetest, most appealing voice: 'Nonna, tell me a story.' The nonna looked at her and smiled.

She said that she could not just tell a story at the drop of a hat. She needed to be in the mood, the right atmosphere. She had to think about it, unless Erica wanted a story from a book, which she could read for her.

'No, Nonna,' Erica said, 'I want one of your stories, I love your stories.' The nonna hugged her again and said she would tell her a story later.

The child sprang up and went off. She wanted what she wanted right now. The nonna smiled. She was like that, her granddaughter, one minute in a huff, next minute all had passed, full of life and happiness and laughter.

After the cleaning of the kitchen was over, all the family went their various ways: some to rest, others to watch a film, others to spend the afternoon at the local bar for non-stop gossip or to play a game of cards.

The woman made her way upstairs; the house was cool and dark, all the shutters closed to keep the afternoon sun out. She walked into her bedroom and took off her sandals to walk on the tiled floor. In the bathroom, she washed her hands and face: the cold water was a delight. She sat on the bed, picking up a book which was on the bedside cabinet. She lay down to have a read. 'Ah lovely,' she thought as she stretched her back on the firm mattress.

'IT'S STORY TIME!' Erica sprang from the other side of the bed her arms stretched up to the sky as she laughed and shouted: 'It's story time!' She had been lying in wait for her Nonna. She jumped on the bed as they laughed. Once they had calmed down and the child lay close to her nonna, she asked if she was in the mood to tell her a story now – was the atmosphere right?

'Yes,' said the nonna. She would tell her a story.

The shutters were closed, the room was dark and cool with a sliver of light coming through. The atmosphere was right.

'Once upon a time, there was a girl who lived high up on the side of a mountain...' she began.

Luath Press Limited

committed to publishing well written books worth reading

LUATH PRESS takes its name from Robert Burns, whose little collie Luath (*Gael.*, swift or nimble) tripped up Jean Armour at a wedding and gave him the chance to speak to the woman who was to be his wife and the abiding love of his life. Burns called one of the 'Twa Dogs' Luath after Cuchullin's hunting dog in Ossian's *Fingal*.

Luath Press was established in 1981 in the heart of Burns country, and is now based a few steps up the road from Burns' first lodgings on Edinburgh's Royal Mile. Luath offers you distinctive writing with a hint of unexpected pleasures.

Most bookshops in the UK, the US, Canada, Australia, New Zealand and parts of Europe, either carry our books in stock or can order them for you. To order direct from us, please send a £sterling cheque, postal order, international money order or your credit card details (number, address of cardholder and expiry date) to us at the address below. Please add post and packing as follows: UK – £1.00 per delivery address; overseas surface mail – £2.50 per delivery address; overseas airmail – £3.50 for the first book to each delivery address, plus £1.00 for each additional book by airmail to the same address. If your order is a gift, we will happily enclose your card or message at no extra charge.

Luath Press Limited
543/2 Castlehill
The Royal Mile
Edinburgh EH1 2ND
Scotland
Telephone: +44 (0)131 225 4326 (24 hours)
email: sales@luath. co.uk
Website: www. luath.co.uk